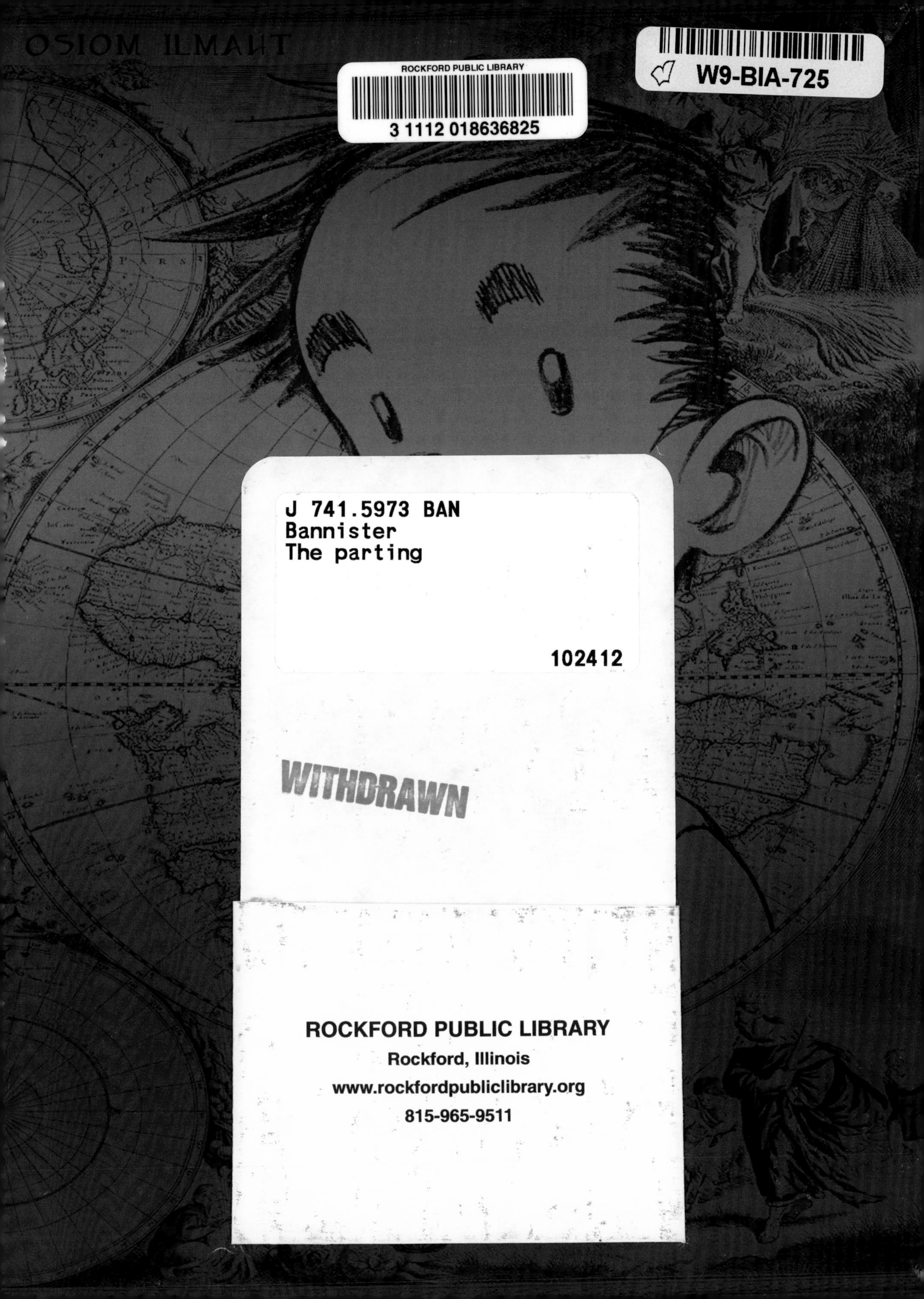

the ElseWhere CHRONICLES

BOOK FIVE
THE PARTING

ART
BANNISTER

STORY
NYKKO

COLORS
JAFFRÉ

GRAPHIC UNIVERSE™ · MINNEAPOLIS · NEW YORK

Thank you to Naïko, M. Reynes, V. Vernay, B. Feroumont, Z. Giallongo, D. Pose, S. Hamaker, and J. P. Ahonen, whose advice is always à propos.

—Banni

To all of my family and to Andrée, for always and forever.

—Nykko

To Mathilde and my parents.

—Jaffré

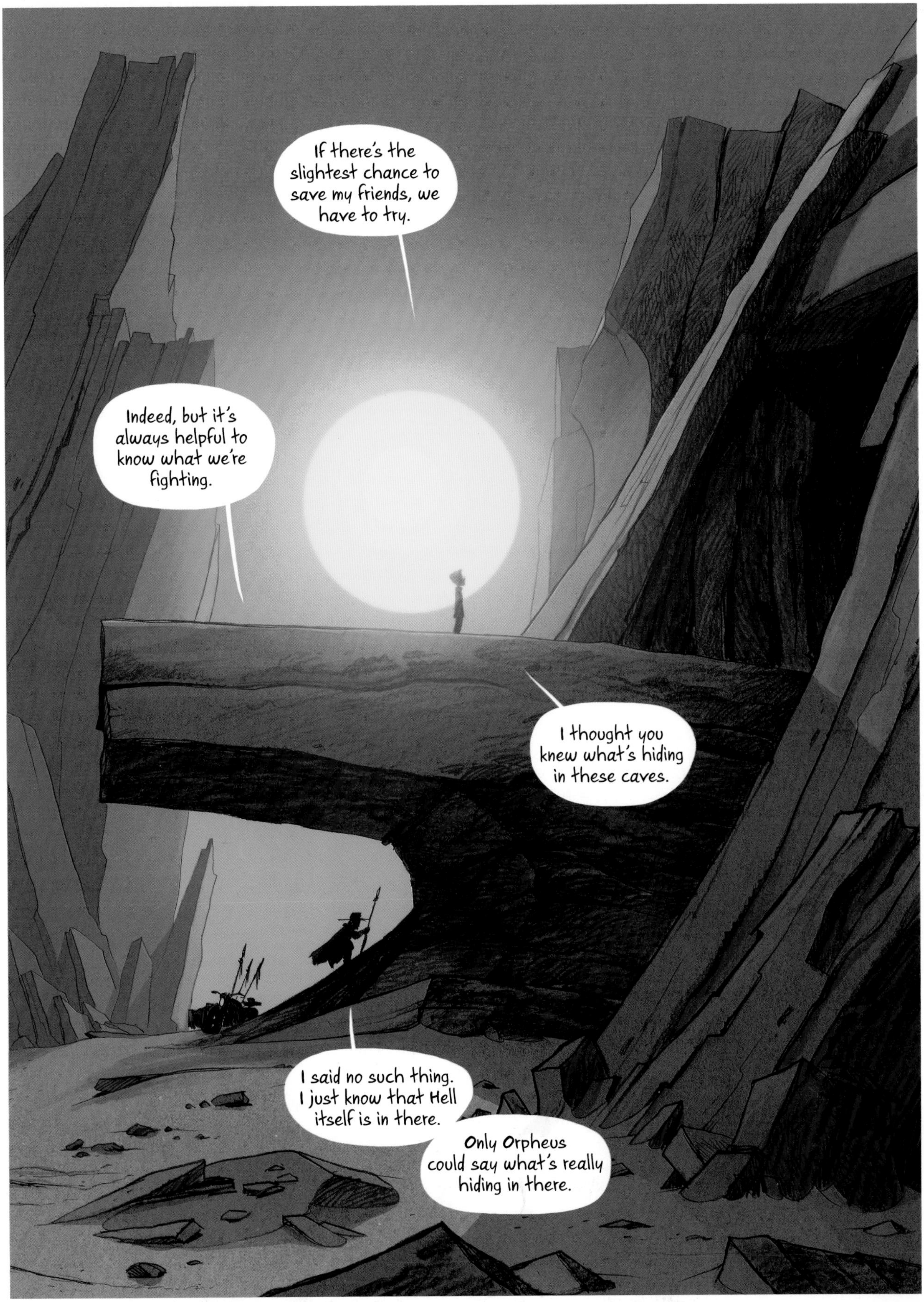
If there's the slightest chance to save my friends, we have to try.
Indeed, but it's always helpful to know what we're fighting.
I thought you knew what's hiding in these caves.
I said no such thing. I just know that Hell itself is in there.
Only Orpheus could say what's really hiding in there.

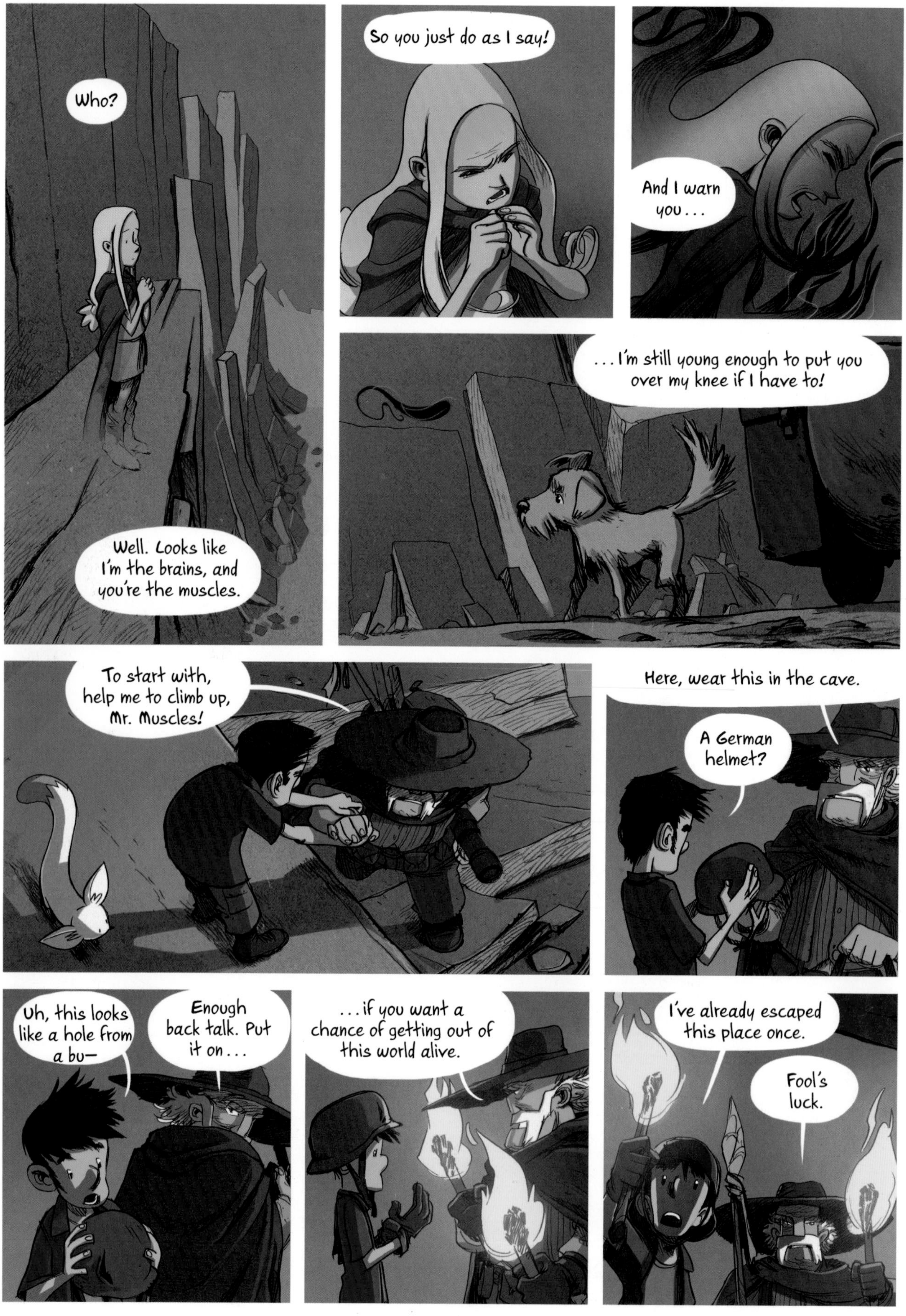
Who?
Well. Looks like I'm the brains, and you're the muscles.
So you just do as I say!
And I warn you . . .
. . . I'm still young enough to put you over my knee if I have to!
To start with, help me to climb up, Mr. Muscles!
Here, wear this in the cave.
A German helmet?
Uh, this looks like a hole from a bu—
Enough back talk. Put it on . . .
. . . if you want a chance of getting out of this world alive.
I've already escaped this place once.
Fool's luck.

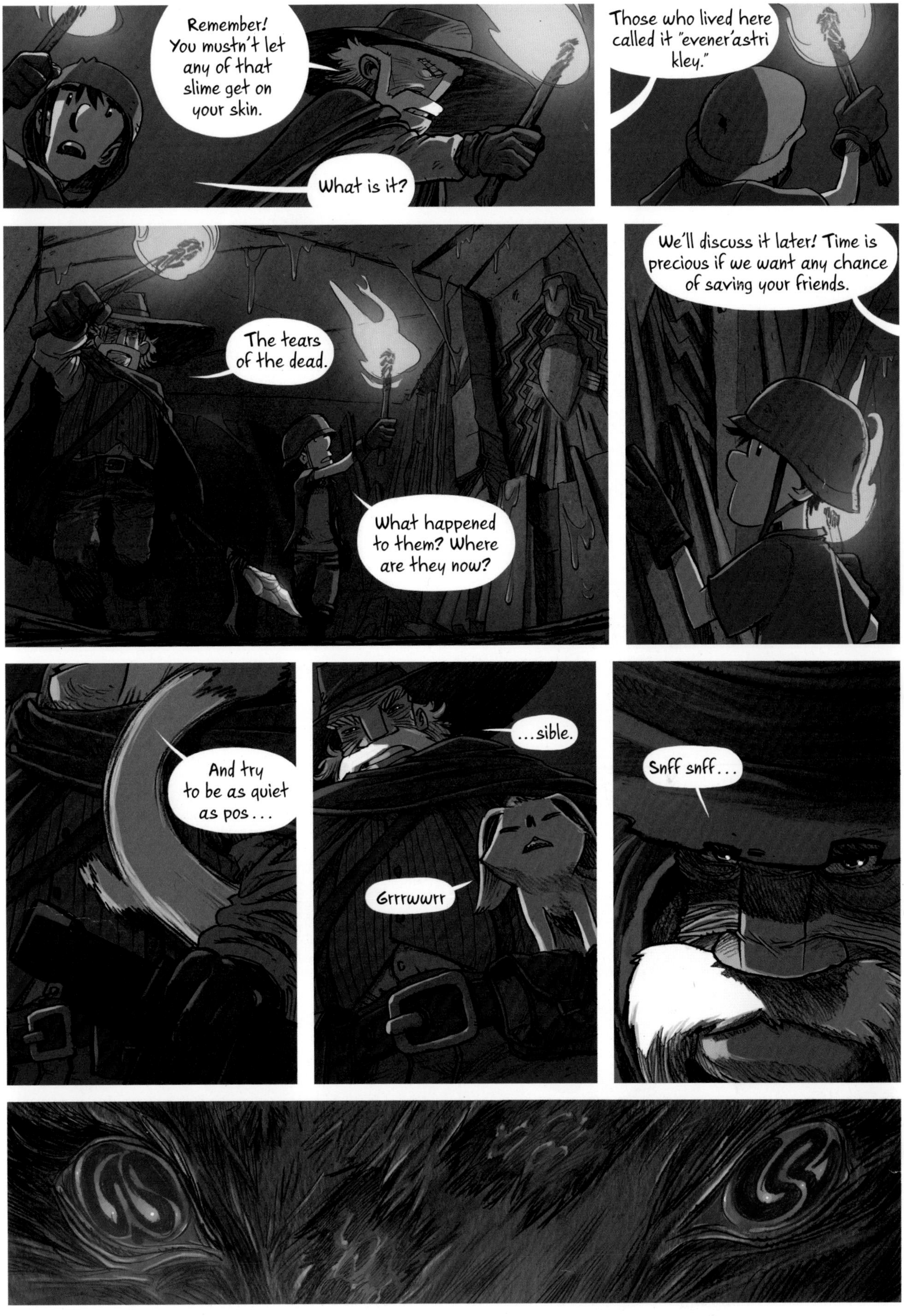
Remember! You mustn't let any of that slime get on your skin.
What is it?
Those who lived here called it "evener'astri kley."
The tears of the dead.
What happened to them? Where are they now?
We'll discuss it later! Time is precious if we want any chance of saving your friends.
And try to be as quiet as pos...
...sible.
Grrrwwrr
Snff snff...

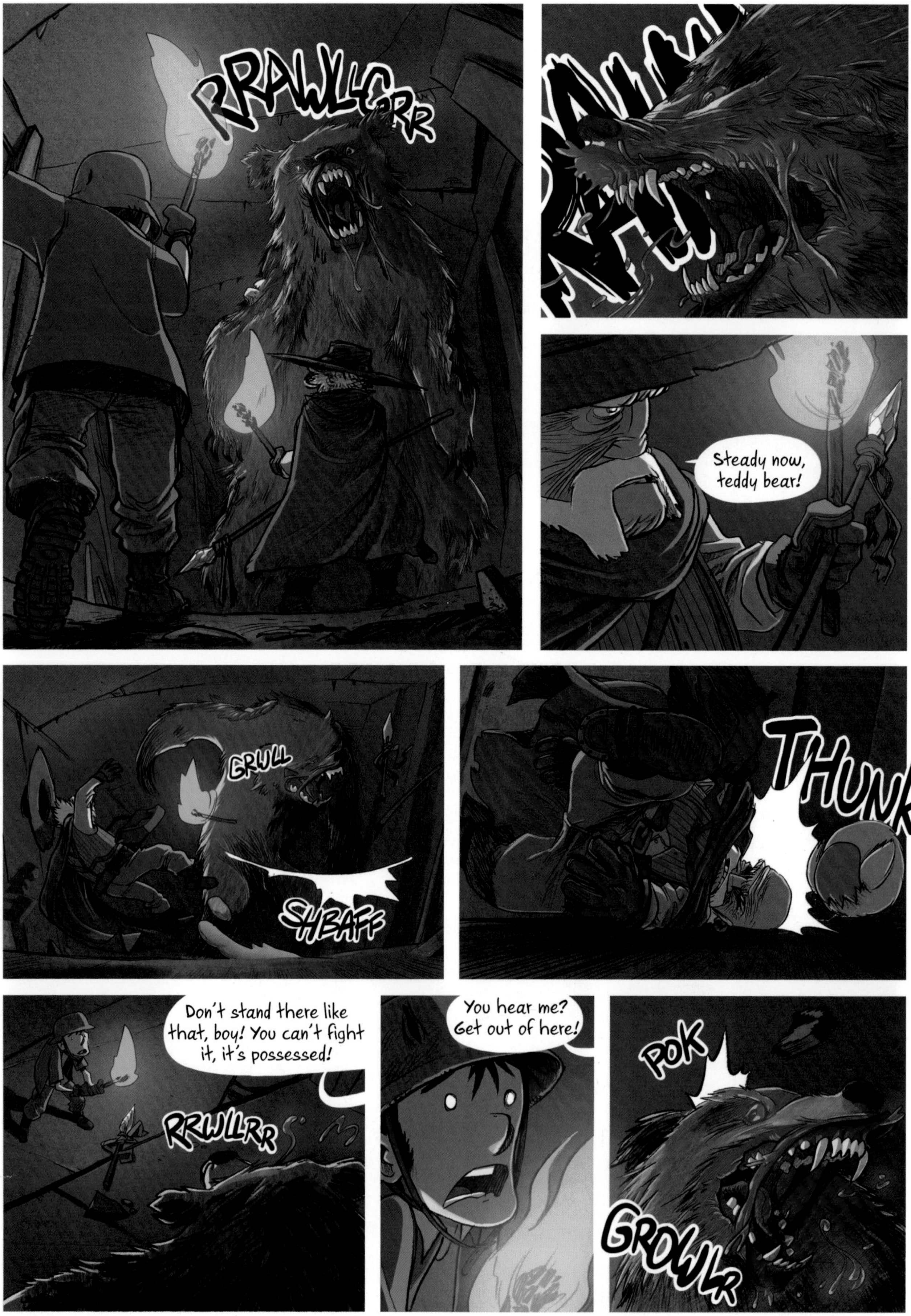
RRAWLLGRRR
Steady now, teddy bear!
GRULL
SHBAFF
THUNK
Don't stand there like that, boy! You can't fight it, it's possessed!
RRWLLRR
You hear me? Get out of here!
POK
GROWLR

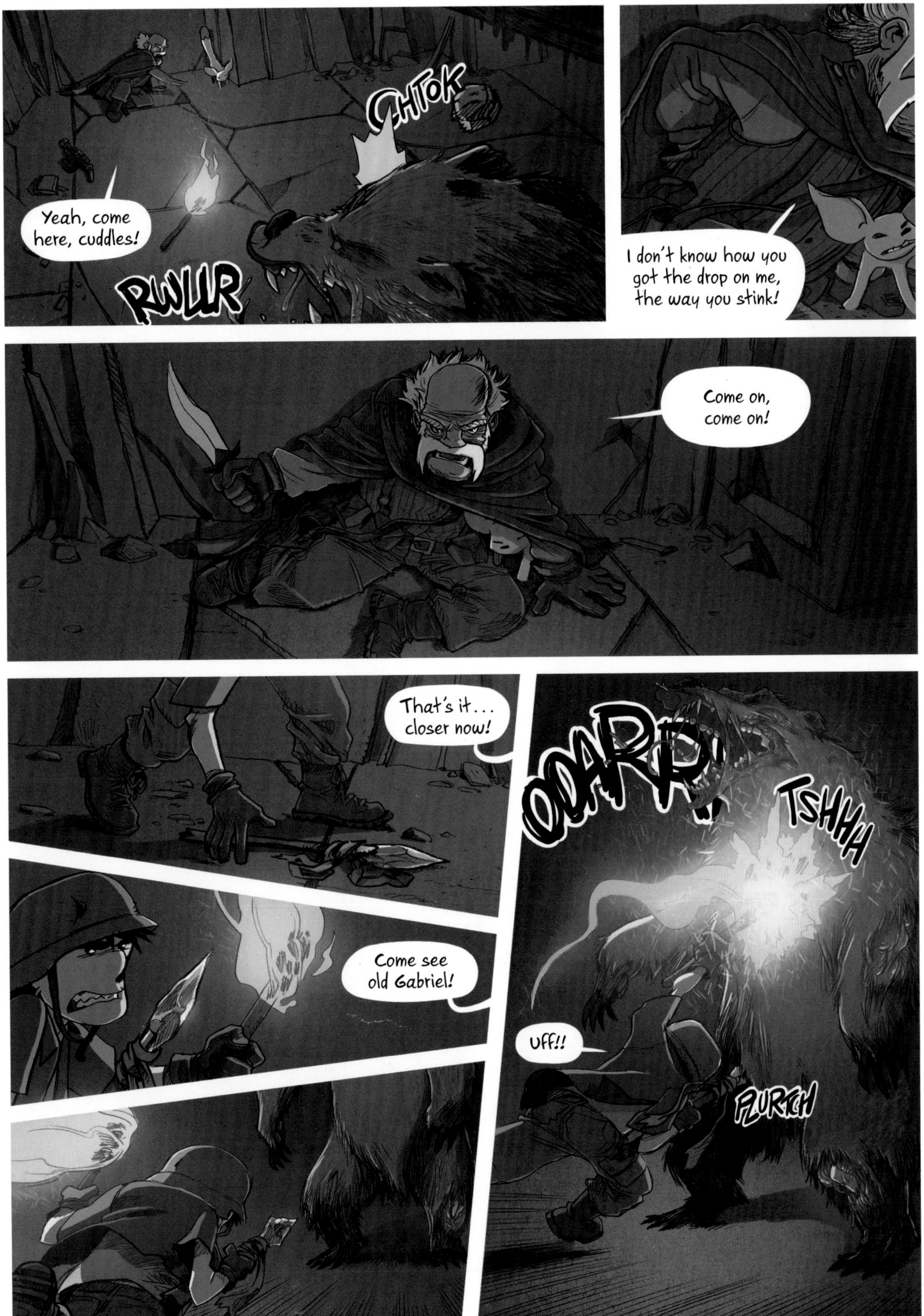
CHTOK
Yeah, come here, cuddles!
RWLLR
I don't know how you got the drop on me, the way you stink!
Come on, come on!
That's it... closer now!
Come see old Gabriel!
OOARR!
TSHHH
UFF!!
FLURTCH

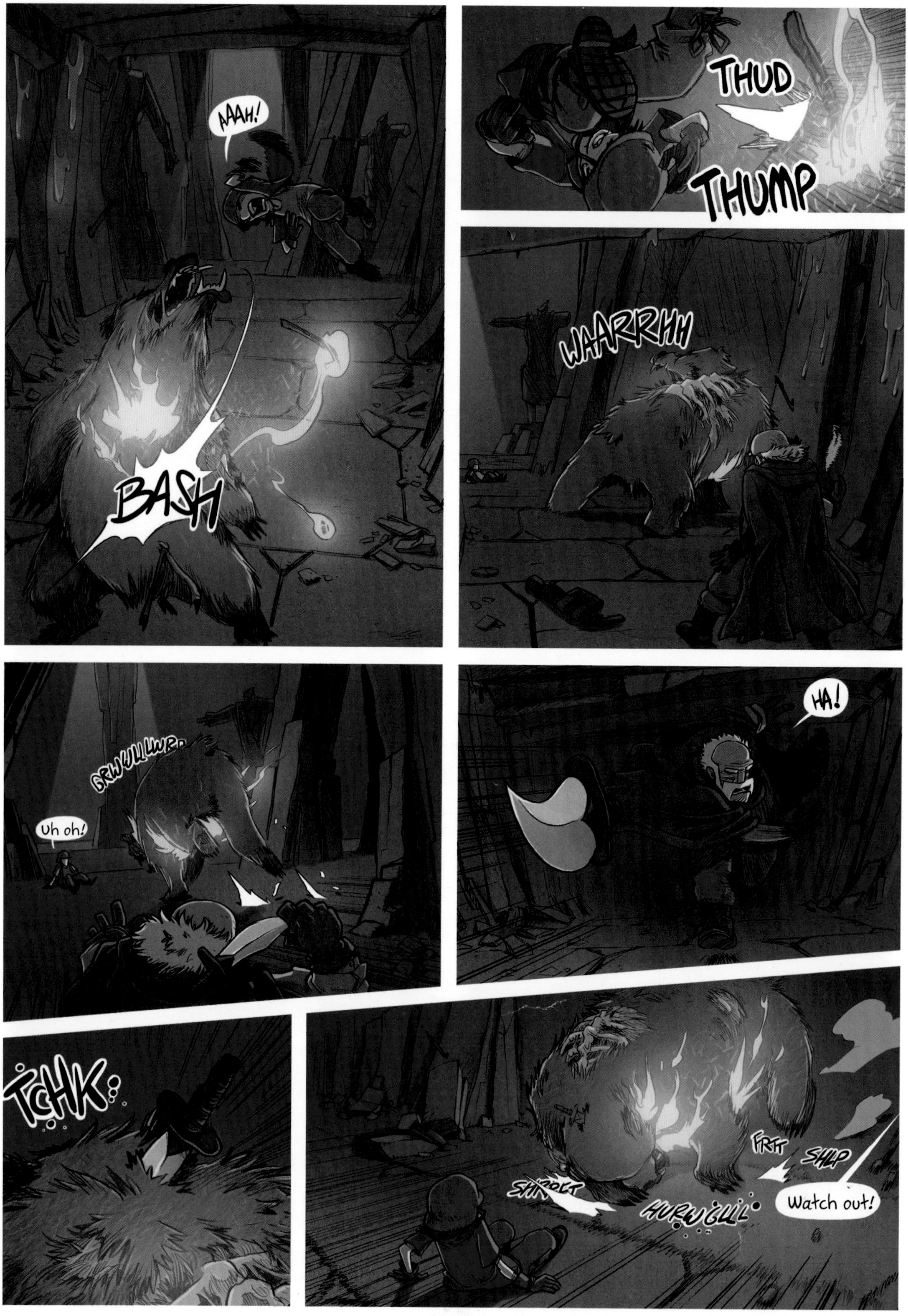
AAAH!
BASH
THUD
THUMP
WAARRHH
GRWULLWRR
Uh oh!
HA!
TCHK
FRTT
SHLP
HURWGLL
Watch out!

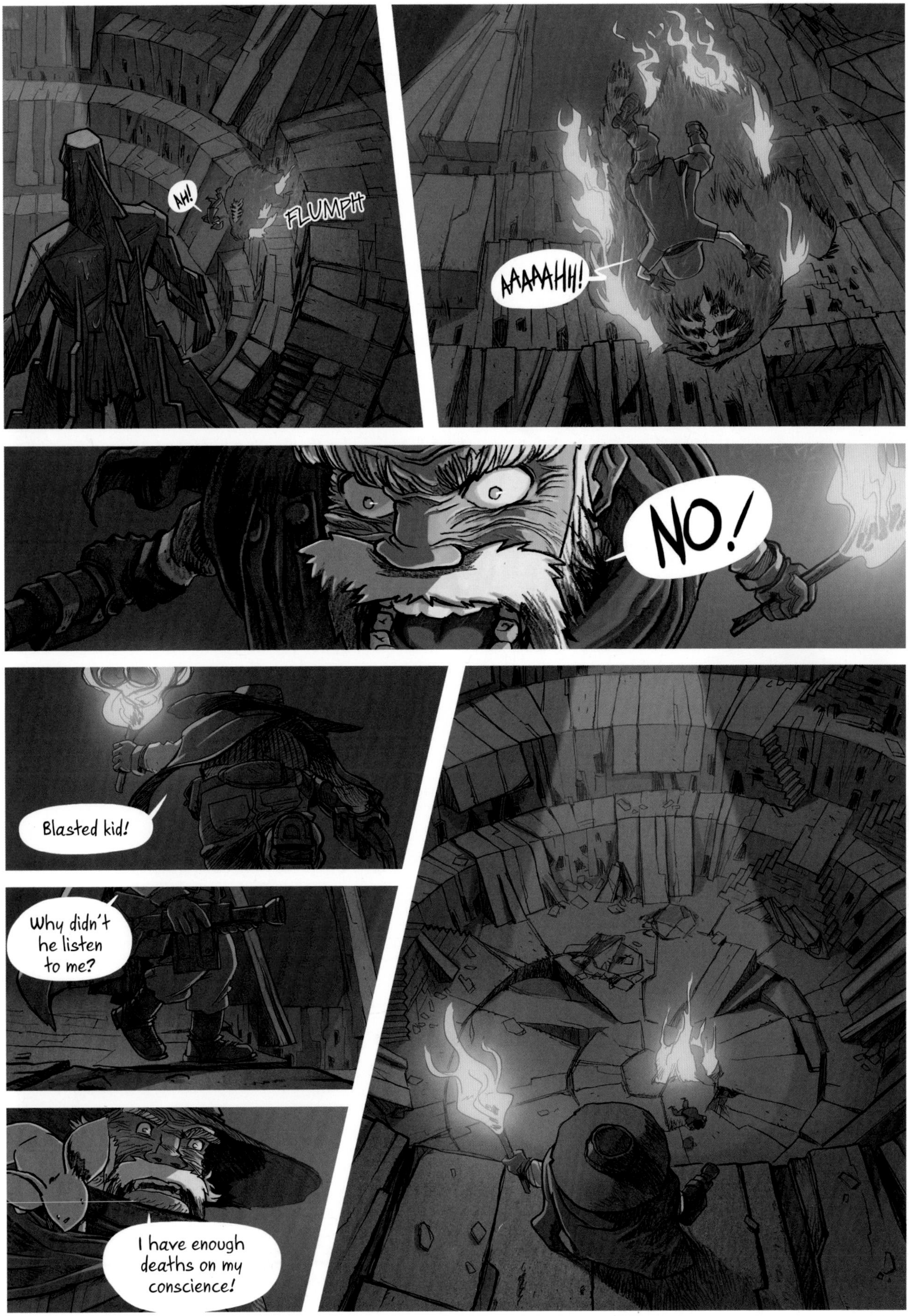
AH!
FLUMPH
AAAAAHH!
NO!
Blasted kid!
Why didn't he listen to me?
I have enough deaths on my conscience!

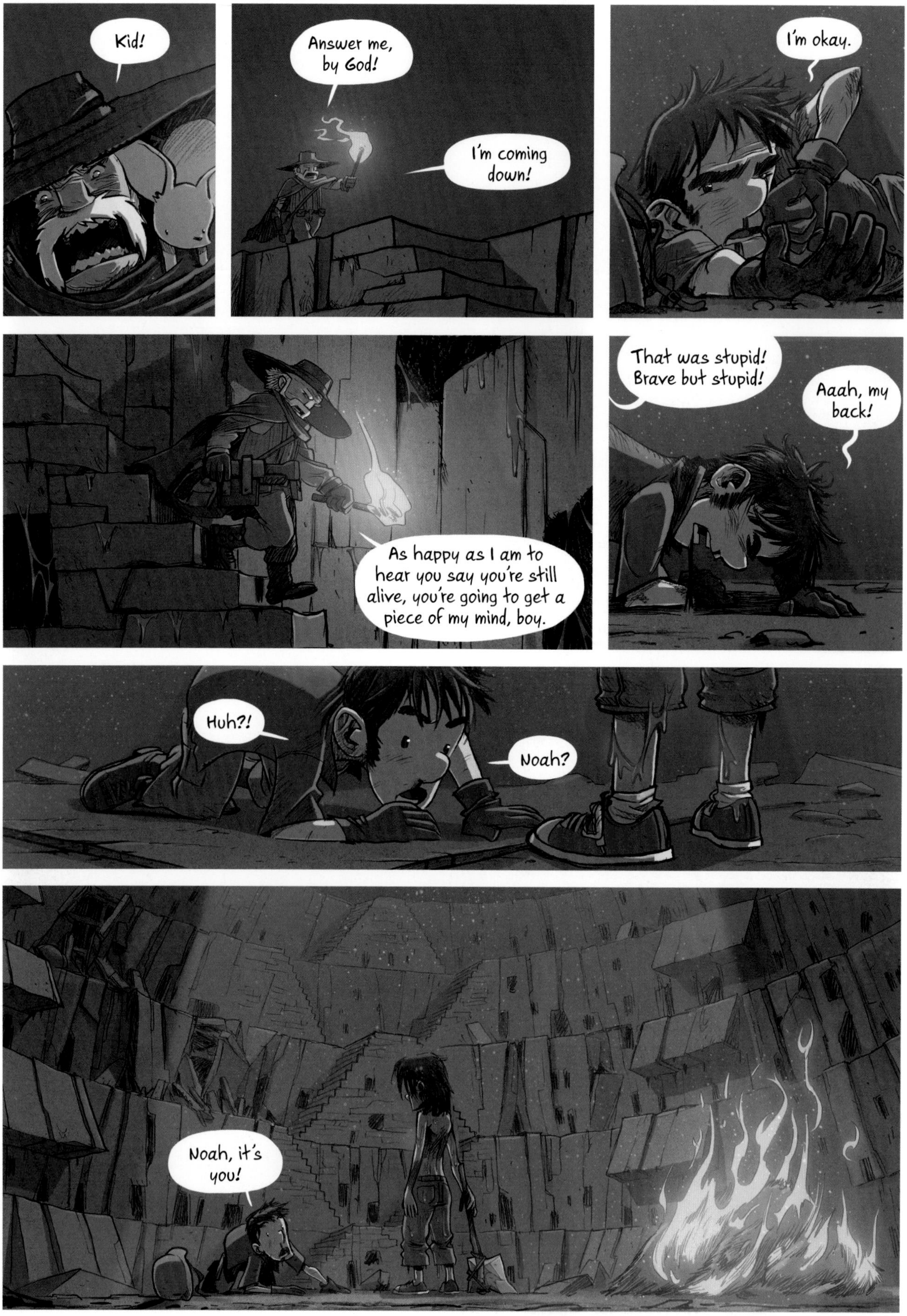
Kid!
Answer me, by God!
I'm coming down!
I'm okay.
As happy as I am to hear you say you're still alive, you're going to get a piece of my mind, boy.
That was stupid! Brave but stupid!
Aaah, my back!
Huh?!
Noah?
Noah, it's you!

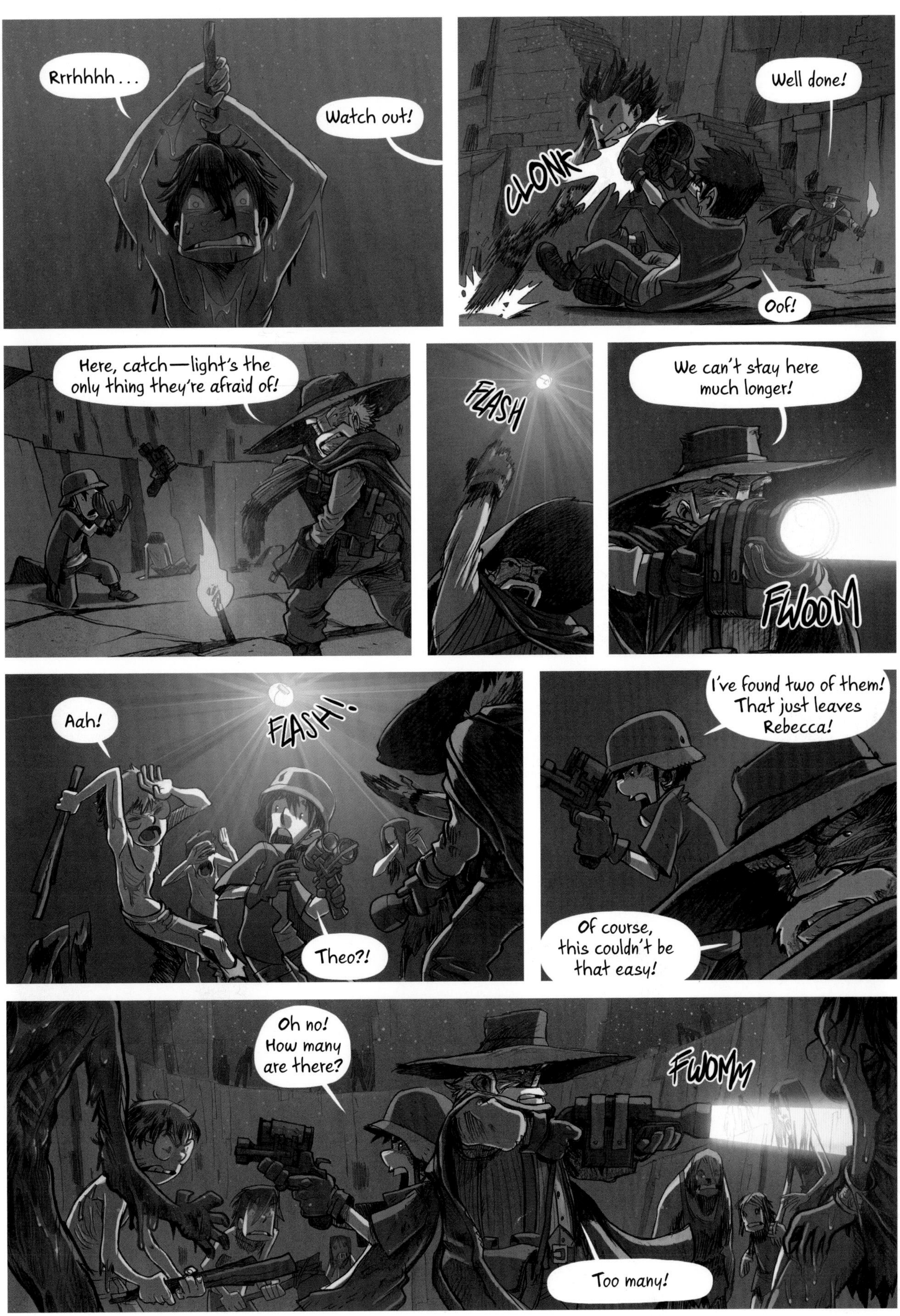
Rrrhhhh...
Watch out!
CLONK
Well done!
Oof!
Here, catch—light's the only thing they're afraid of!
FLASH
We can't stay here much longer!
FWOOM
Aah!
FLASH!
Theo?!
I've found two of them! That just leaves Rebecca!
Of course, this couldn't be that easy!
Oh no! How many are there?
FWOMM
Too many!

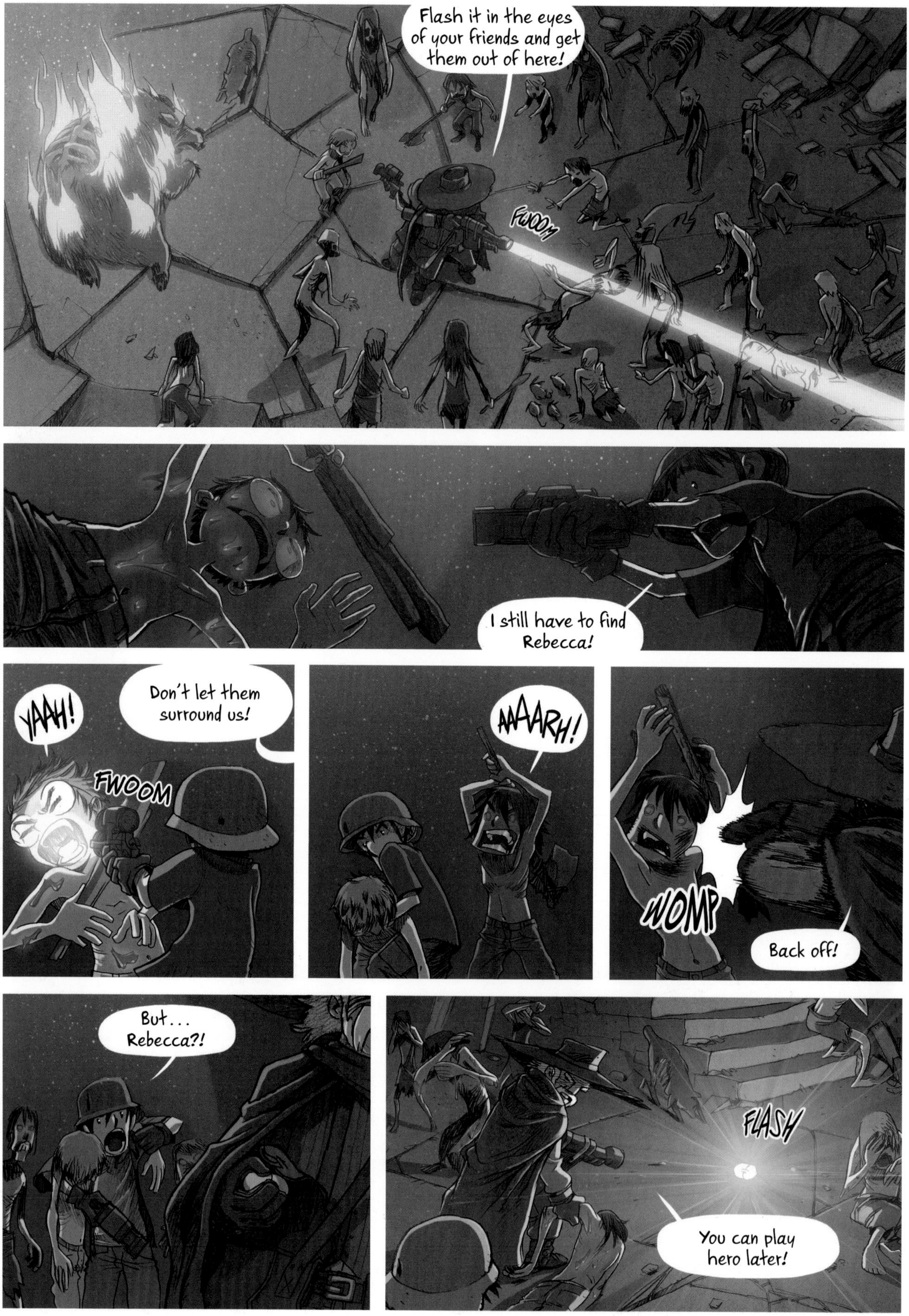
Flash it in the eyes of your friends and get them out of here!
FWOOM
I still have to find Rebecca!
YAAH!
Don't let them surround us!
FWOOM
AAAARH!
WOMP
Back off!
But... Rebecca?!
FLASH
You can play hero later!

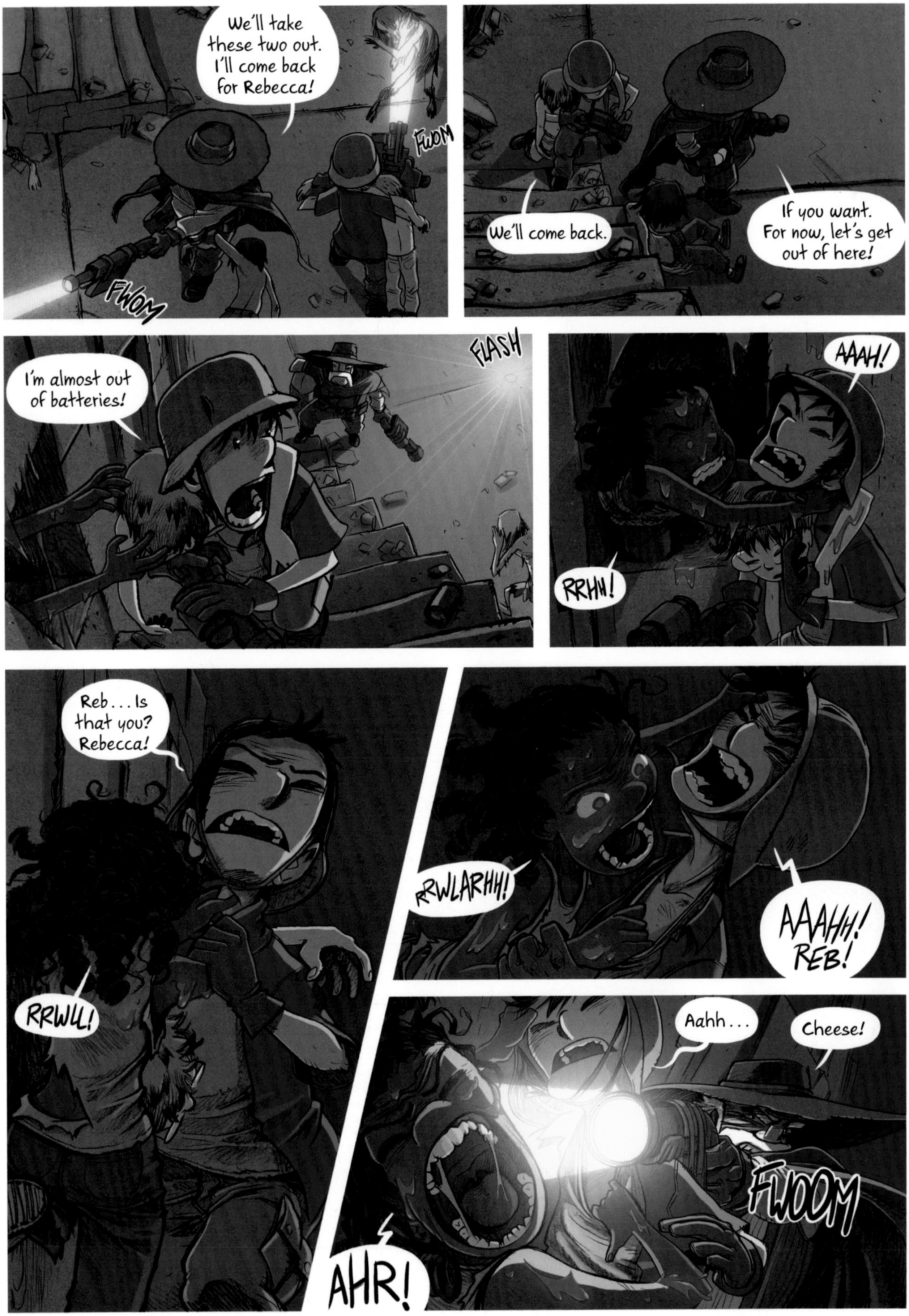
We'll take these two out. I'll come back for Rebecca!
FWOOM
FWOM
We'll come back.
If you want. For now, let's get out of here!
I'm almost out of batteries!
FLASH
AAAH!
RRHH!
Reb... Is that you? Rebecca!
RRWLL!
RRWLARHH!
AAAHH! REB!
Aahh...
Cheese!
FWOOM
AHR!

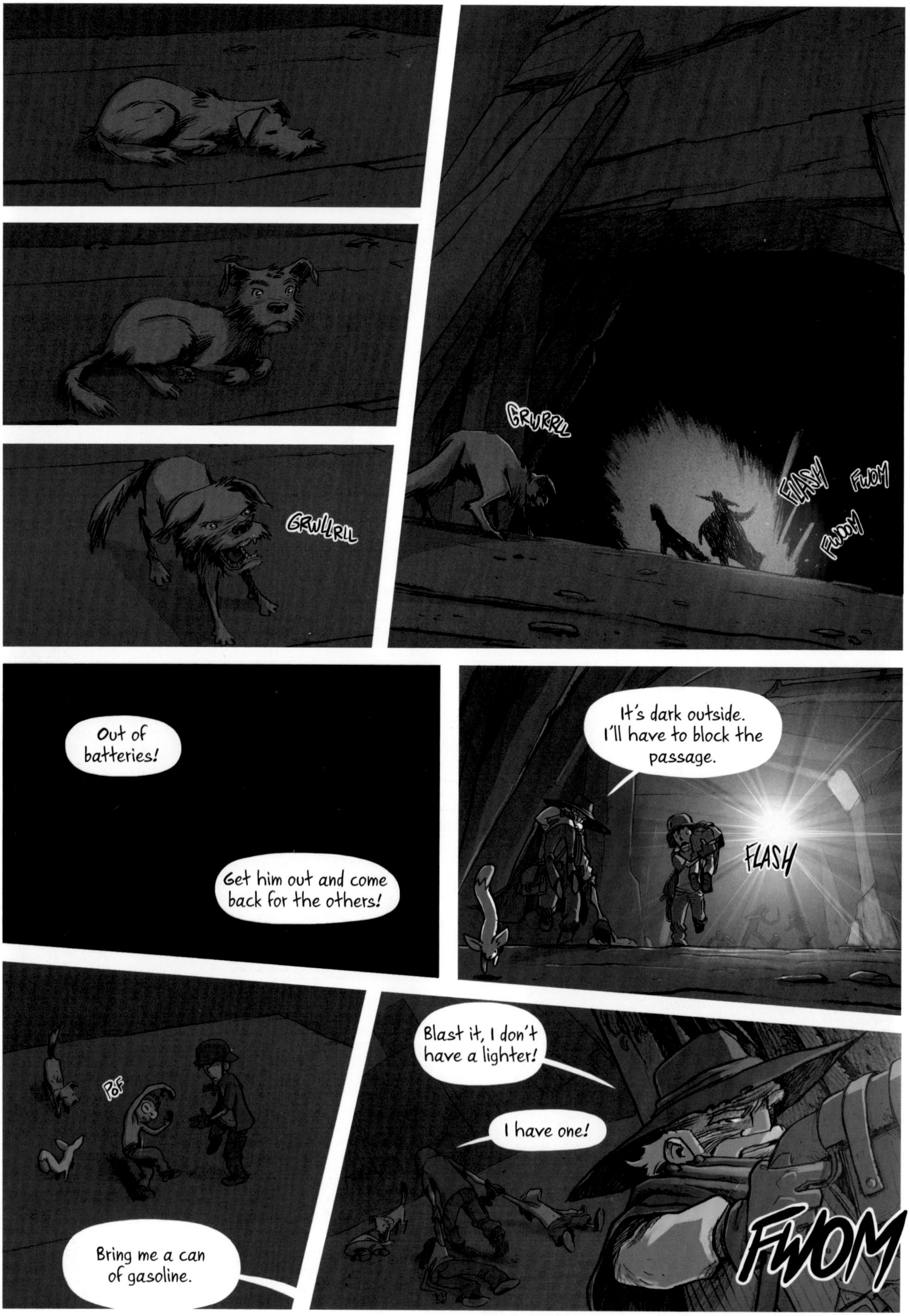
GRWLLRLL
GRWRRLL
FLASH
FWOM
FWOOM
Out of batteries!
Get him out and come back for the others!
It's dark outside. I'll have to block the passage.
FLASH
POF
Bring me a can of gasoline.
Blast it, I don't have a lighter!
I have one!
FWOM

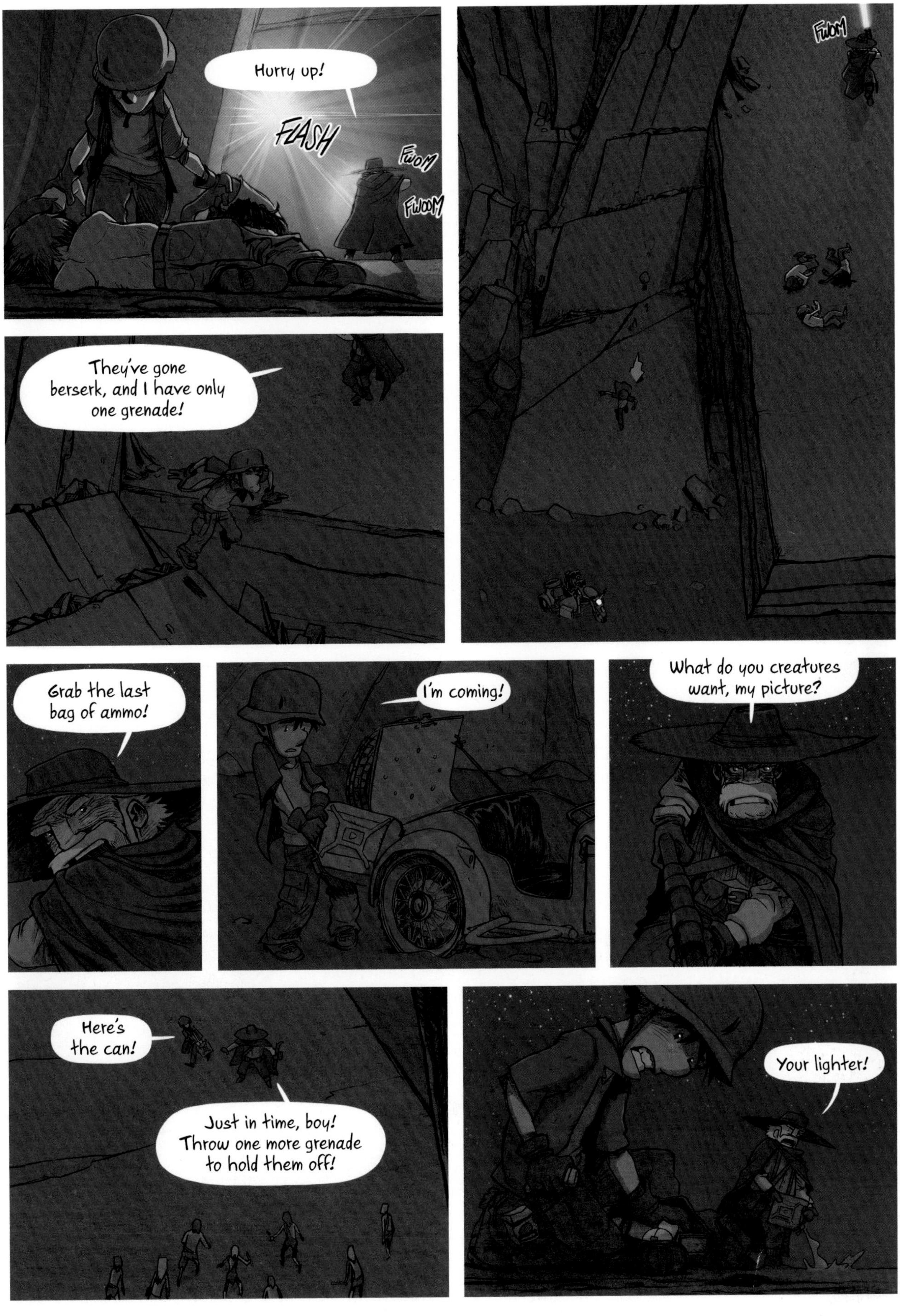
Hurry up!
FLASH
FWOM
FWOOM
FWOM
They've gone berserk, and I have only one grenade!
Grab the last bag of ammo!
I'm coming!
What do you creatures want, my picture?
Here's the can!
Just in time, boy! Throw one more grenade to hold them off!
Your lighter!

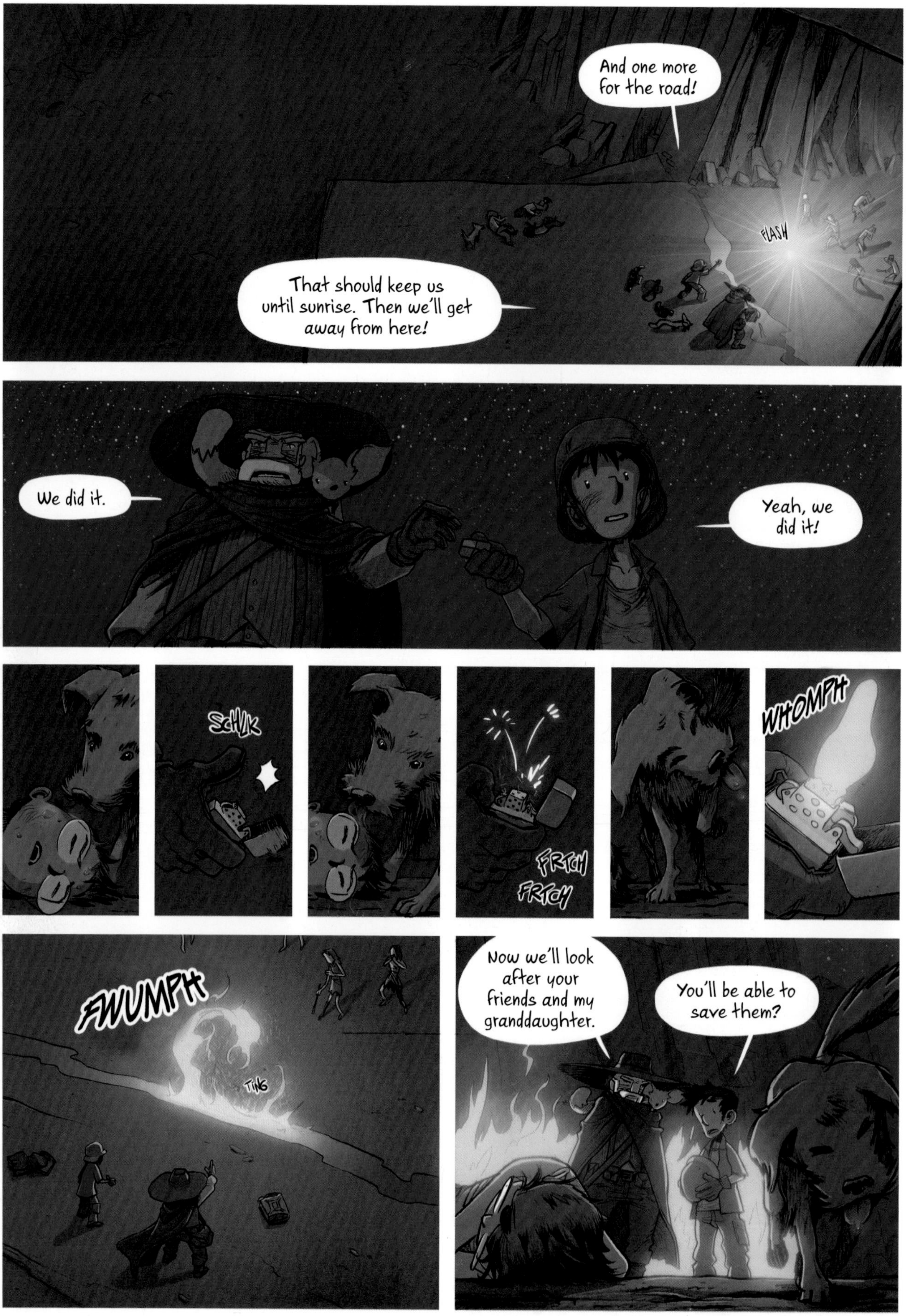
And one more for the road!
FLASH
That should keep us until sunrise. Then we'll get away from here!
We did it.
Yeah, we did it!
SCHLIK
FRTCH
FRTCH
WHOMPH
FWUMPH
TING
Now we'll look after your friends and my granddaughter.
You'll be able to save them?

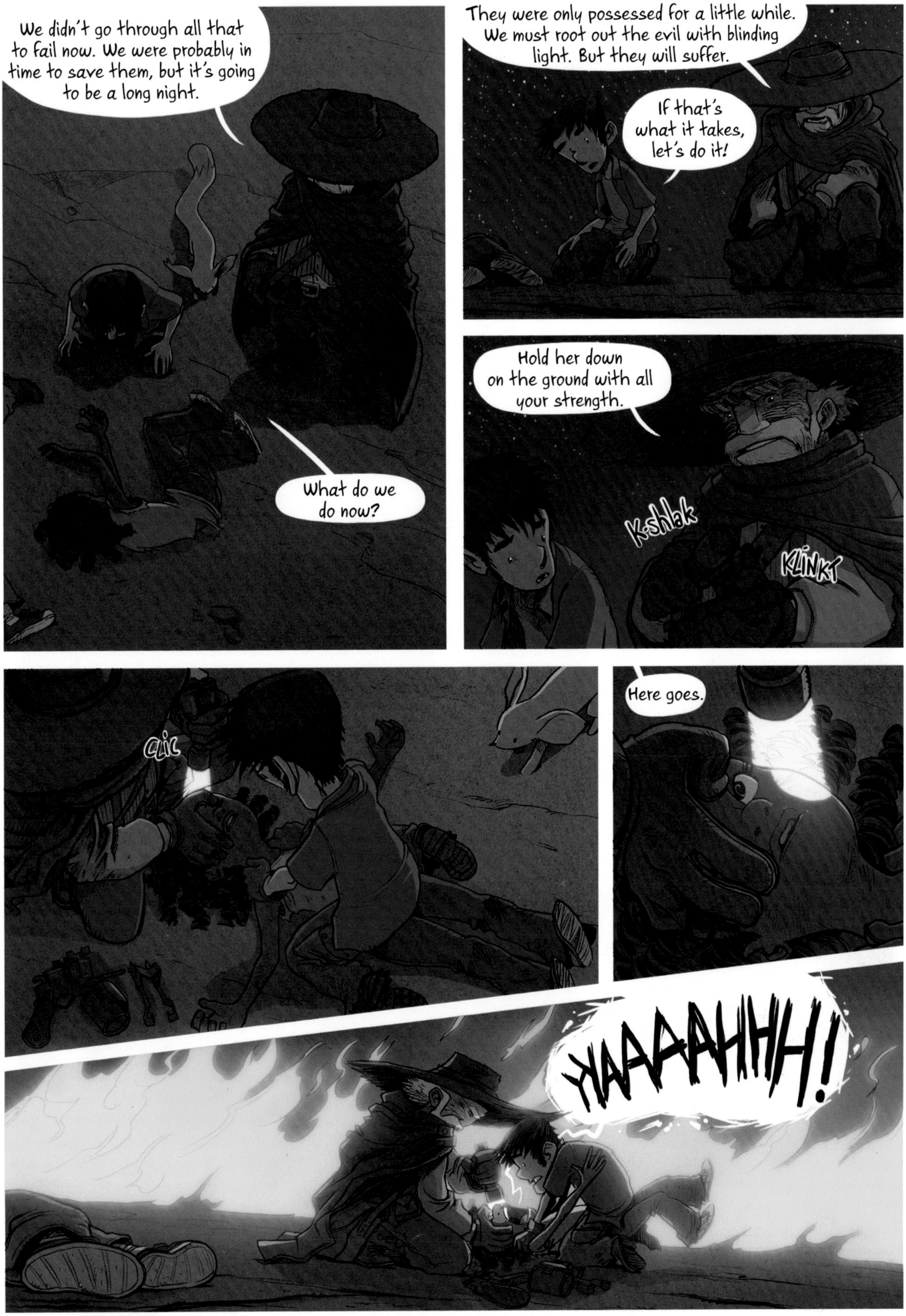
We didn't go through all that to fail now. We were probably in time to save them, but it's going to be a long night.
What do we do now?
They were only possessed for a little while. We must root out the evil with blinding light. But they will suffer.
If that's what it takes, let's do it!
Hold her down on the ground with all your strength.
K-SHLAK
KLINK!
CLIC
Here goes.
YAAAAHHH!

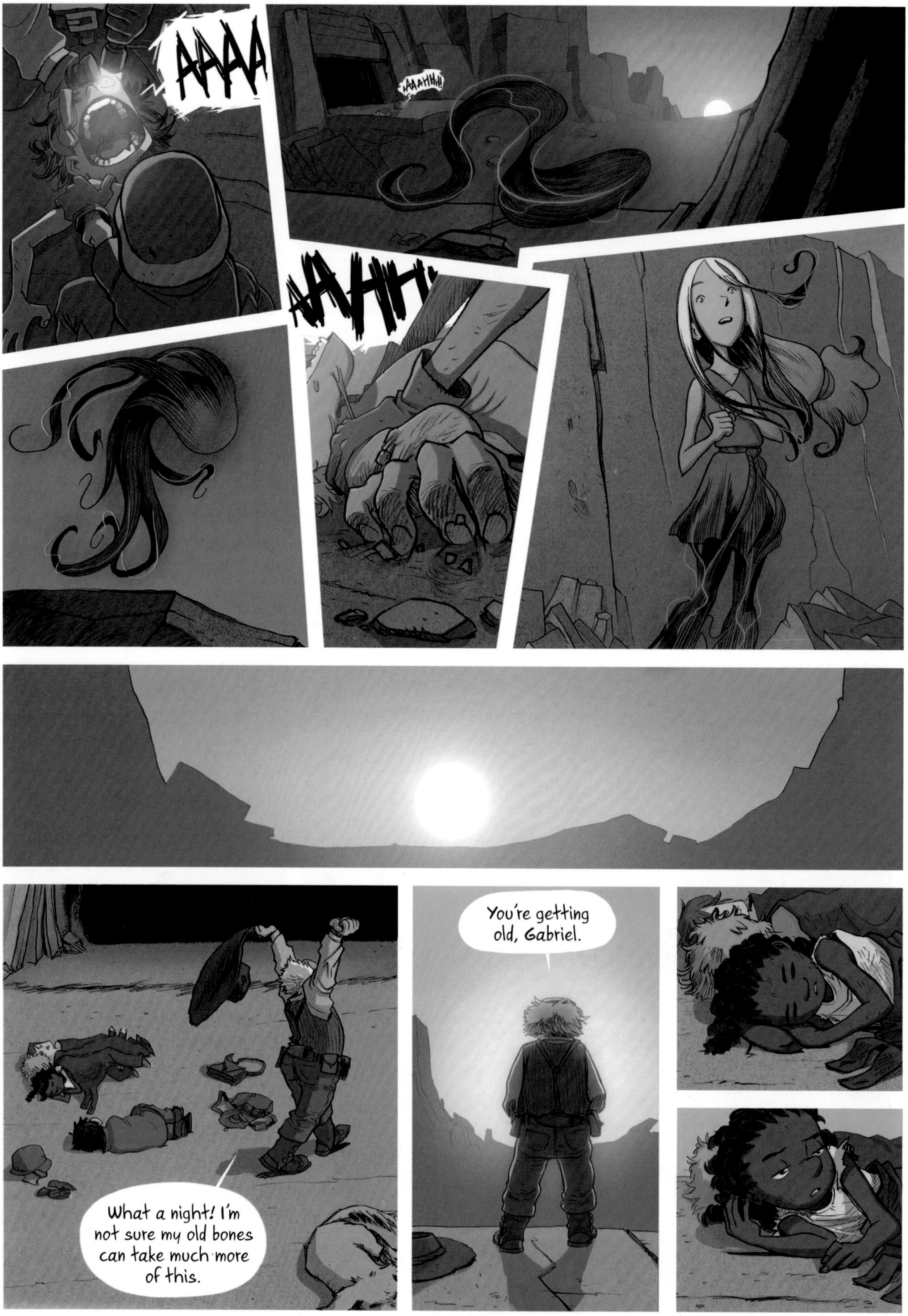
AAAA
AAAHH!
AAHH
You're getting old, Gabriel.
What a night! I'm not sure my old bones can take much more of this.

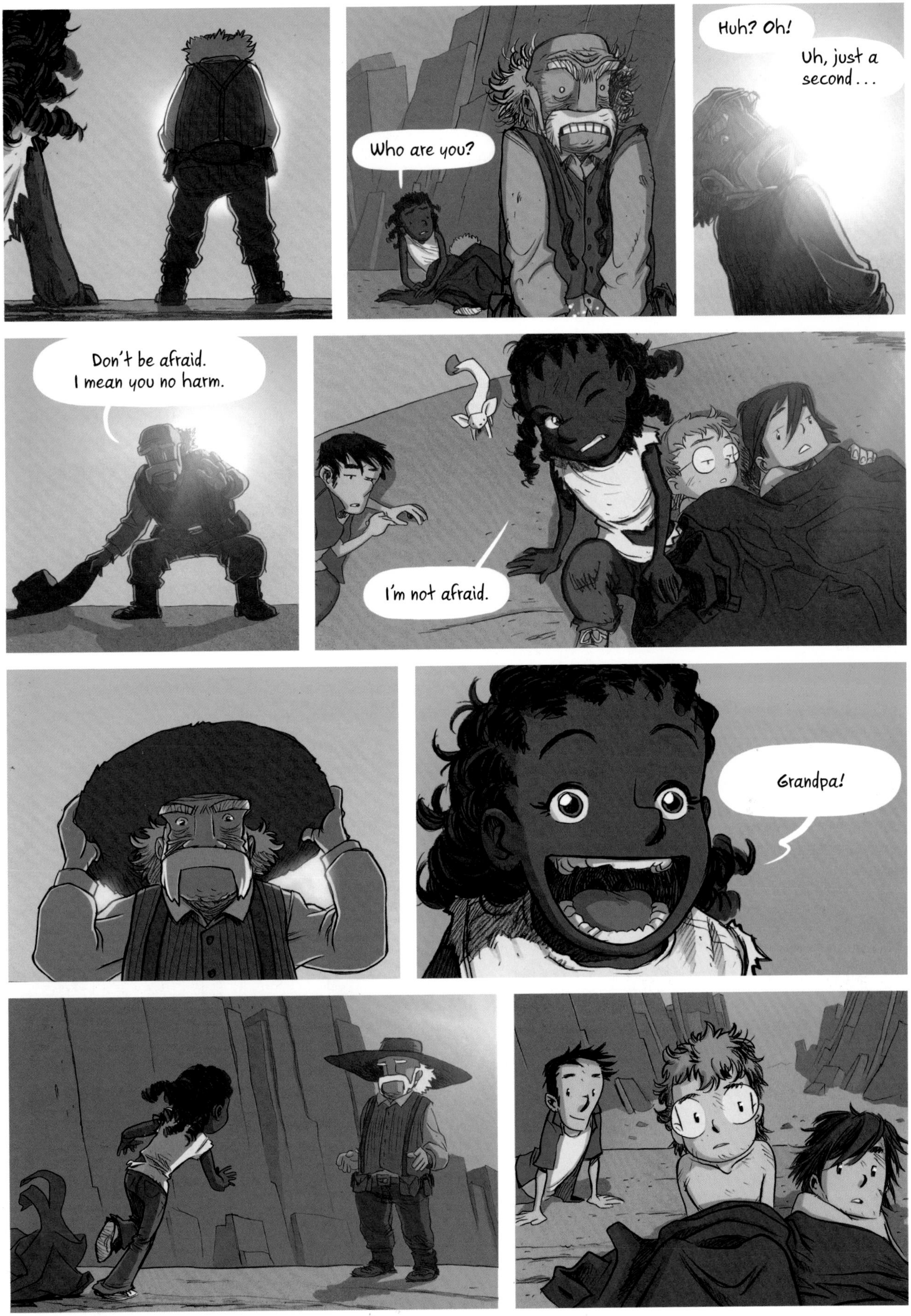
Who are you?
Huh? Oh!
Uh, just a second . . .
Don't be afraid. I mean you no harm.
I'm not afraid.
Grandpa!

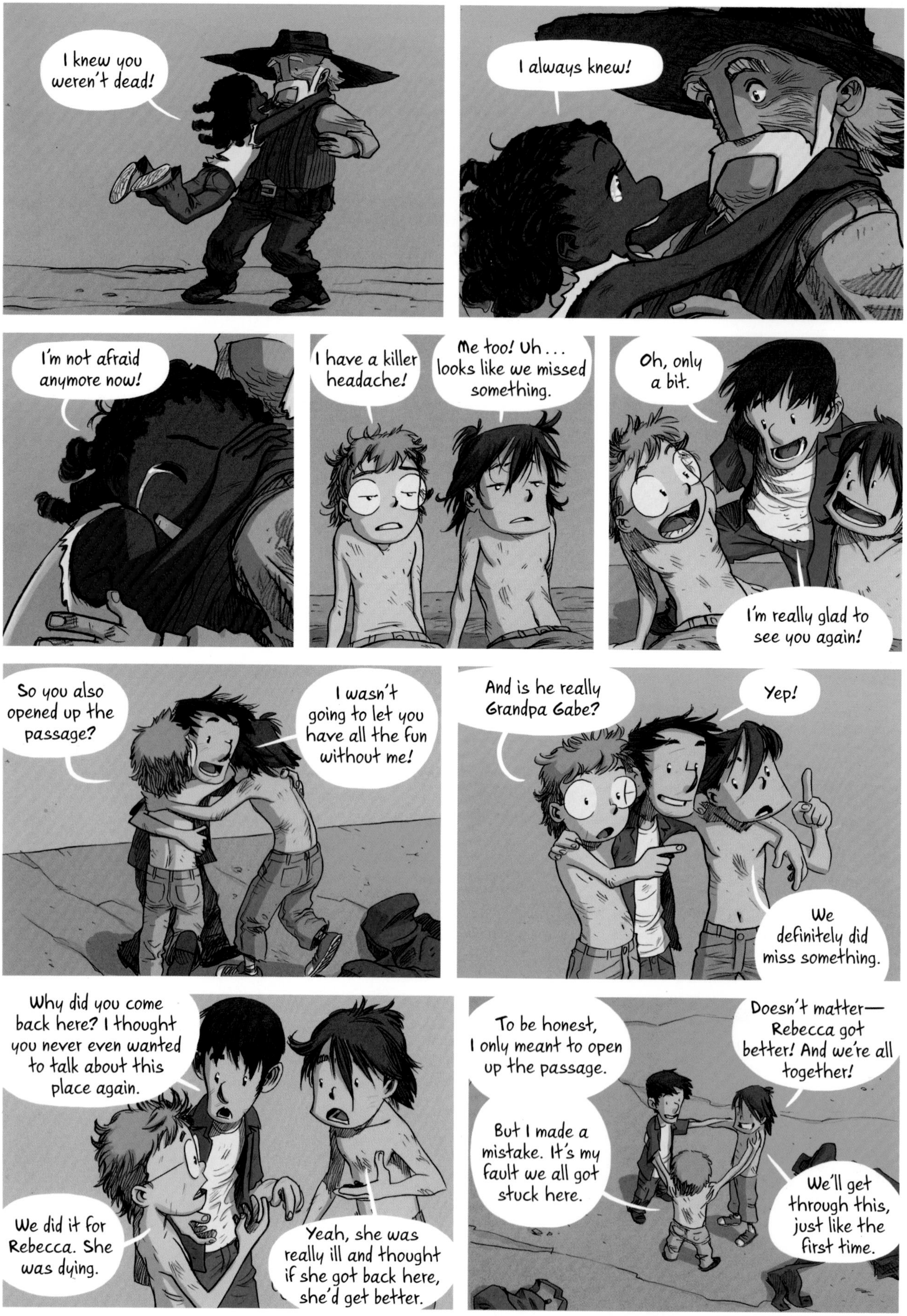
I knew you weren't dead!
I always knew!
I'm not afraid anymore now!
I have a killer headache!
Me too! Uh . . . looks like we missed something.
Oh, only a bit.
I'm really glad to see you again!
So you also opened up the passage?
I wasn't going to let you have all the fun without me!
And is he really Grandpa Gabe?
Yep!
We definitely did miss something.
Why did you come back here? I thought you never even wanted to talk about this place again.
We did it for Rebecca. She was dying.
Yeah, she was really ill and thought if she got back here, she'd get better.
To be honest, I only meant to open up the passage.
But I made a mistake. It's my fault we all got stuck here.
Doesn't matter—Rebecca got better! And we're all together!
We'll get through this, just like the first time.

You know, I thought for a while that you were the Master of Shadows.

What?! Ilvanna guided you?

Actually, it was her ghost! We couldn't touch her, and she didn't speak.

We all know it couldn't have really been Ilvanna.

Of course not. But then what was it?

Noah thinks it's a trap by the Master of Shadows to get Rebecca.

Who else could it be?

But for what reason?

Everything okay, guys?

I was telling Max how Ilvanna lured you here.

It seems like this jerk Master of Shadows was manipulating you.

Maybe not... Since I came here, I haven't been ill anymore.

Ill? You were ill in the other world?

The doctors said I'd die. But Ilvanna came looking for me and saved me.

You were very weak? You suffered terrible headaches and were unable to eat? You trembled and your vision was blurry?

Yes...

It sounds like you've heard of this before.

It could be... Wait a moment, what's that sound?!

Yes, I hear it too!

Whoa, have you seen this bike?

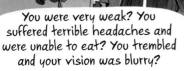

This is just like Indiana Jones!

Come on, let's take a ride!

Oh no...

Get away from there, boy!

Come on! Let's go!

Get away from there, by God, get away!

What's going on?!

Look, something's moving!

It's a sand whale.

No, not one whale. A herd!

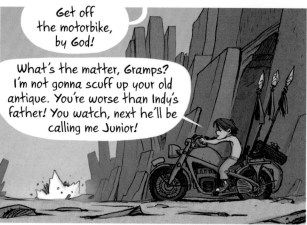

Get off the motorbike, by God!

What's the matter, Gramps? I'm not gonna scuff up your old antique. You're worse than Indy's father! You watch, next he'll be calling me Junior!

Behind you!

Huh? What? I started it up?

BRRRRRRR

RRRRR RR

BRLLRWRRRRR

Oh no, not this again!

Aah!

BRRR   RR

22

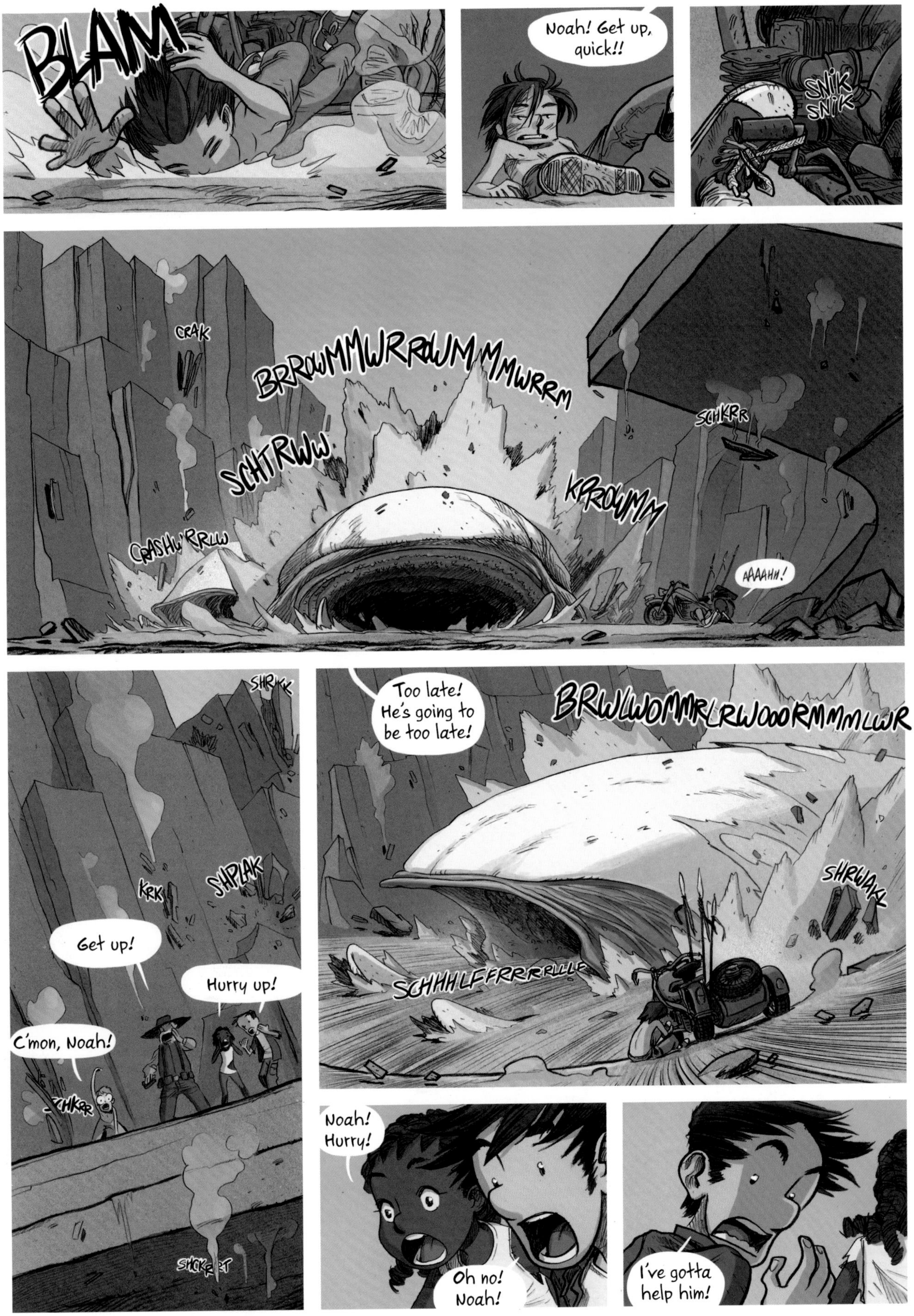
BLAM
Noah! Get up, quick!!
SNIK SNIK
CRAK
BRROWMMWRROWM MMWRRM
SCHTRWW
SCHKRR
KRROWMM
CRASHWRRLW
AAAAHH!
SHRKK
KRK
SHPLAK
Get up!
Hurry up!
C'mon, Noah!
SHKRRT
Too late! He's going to be too late!
BRWLWOMMRLRWOOORMMMLWR
SHRWAKK
SCHHHLFFRRRRLLLF
Noah! Hurry!
Oh no! Noah!
I've gotta help him!

BRRWOOMRRWWM...

SHPRWOOM

SSHLLRRFFM

SPERRTCHH

KRRSH

KRSH

SHPLAK

A rope, I need a rope!

WHOOSH

FRRSSHWRRSH

Forget it, I'm going down there!

SNAP

Hey! What are you doing? Let me go!

It's too late! Sacrificing yourself for your friend would be pointless!

SSHHFR

Maax!

24

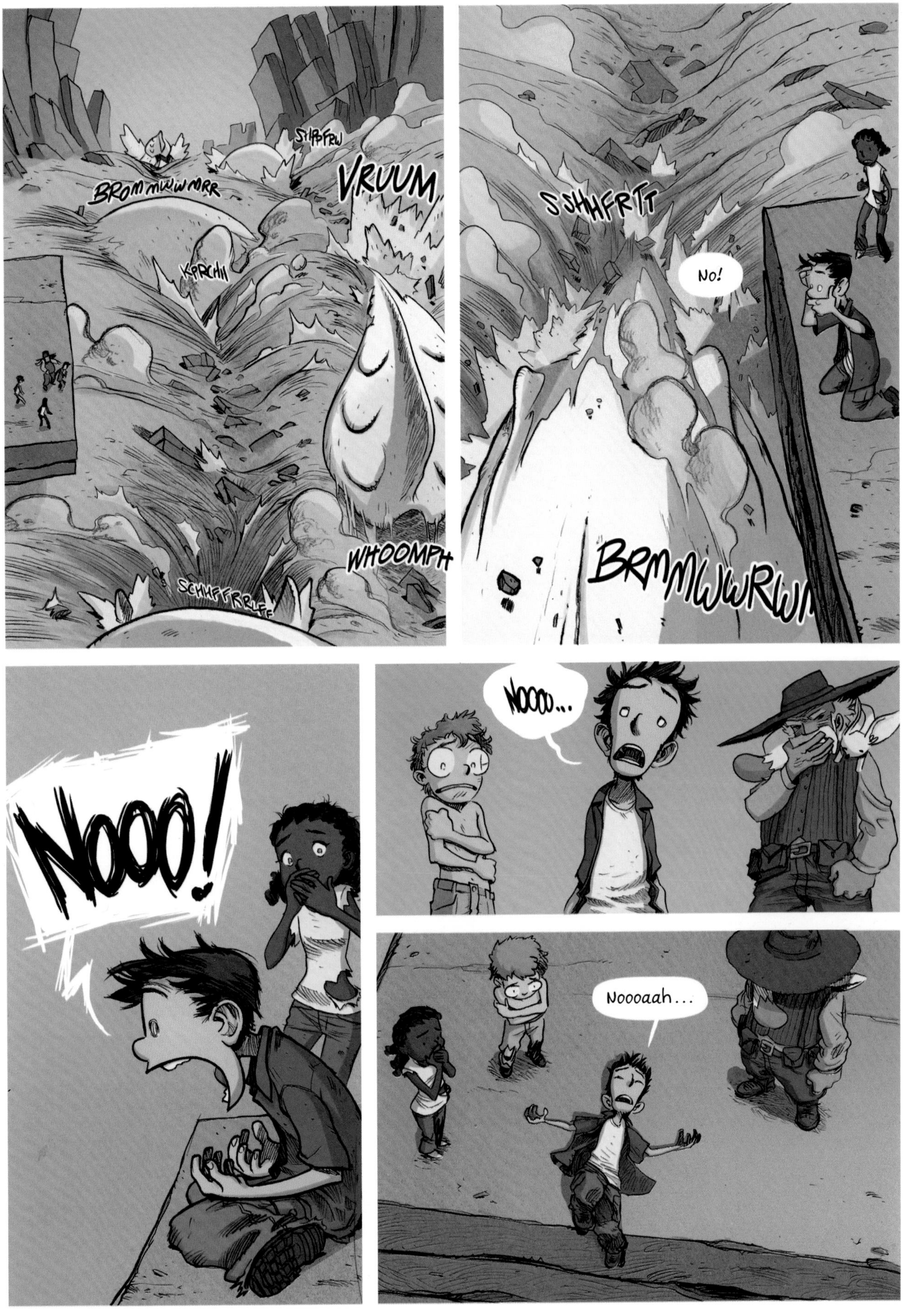
STIPPFRW
BROMMWWMRR
VRUUM
KPRCHH
WHOOMPH
SCHHFFRRLFF
SSHHFRTT
No!
BRMMWWRWN
NOOO!
NOOOO...
Noooaah...

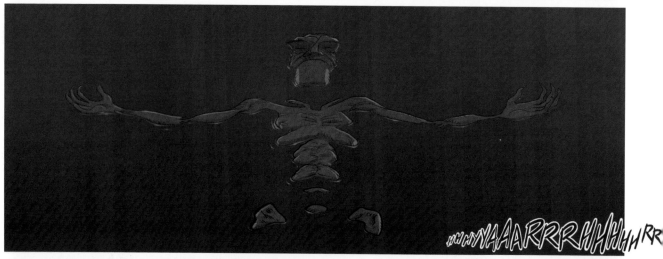

ᵘᴴᶜⁿᵧYAAARRRHHHHₕᵣRR

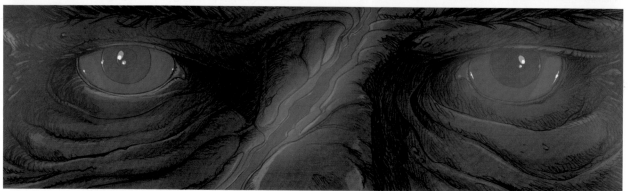

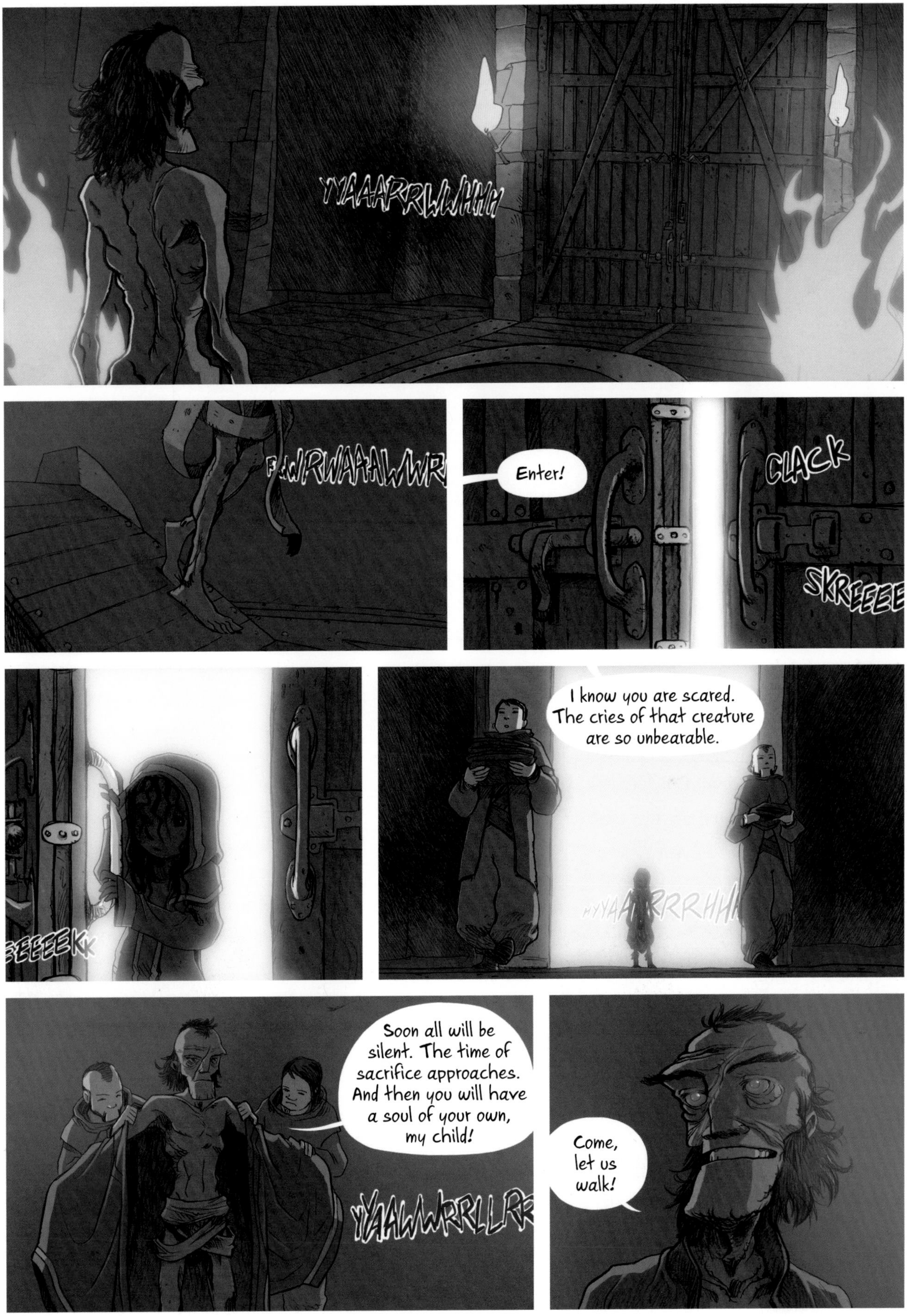
YYAAARRWWHHH
Enter!
CLACK
SKREEEEE
EEEEEKK
I know you are scared. The cries of that creature are so unbearable.
Soon all will be silent. The time of sacrifice approaches. And then you will have a soul of your own, my child!
YYAAWWRRLLRR
Come, let us walk!

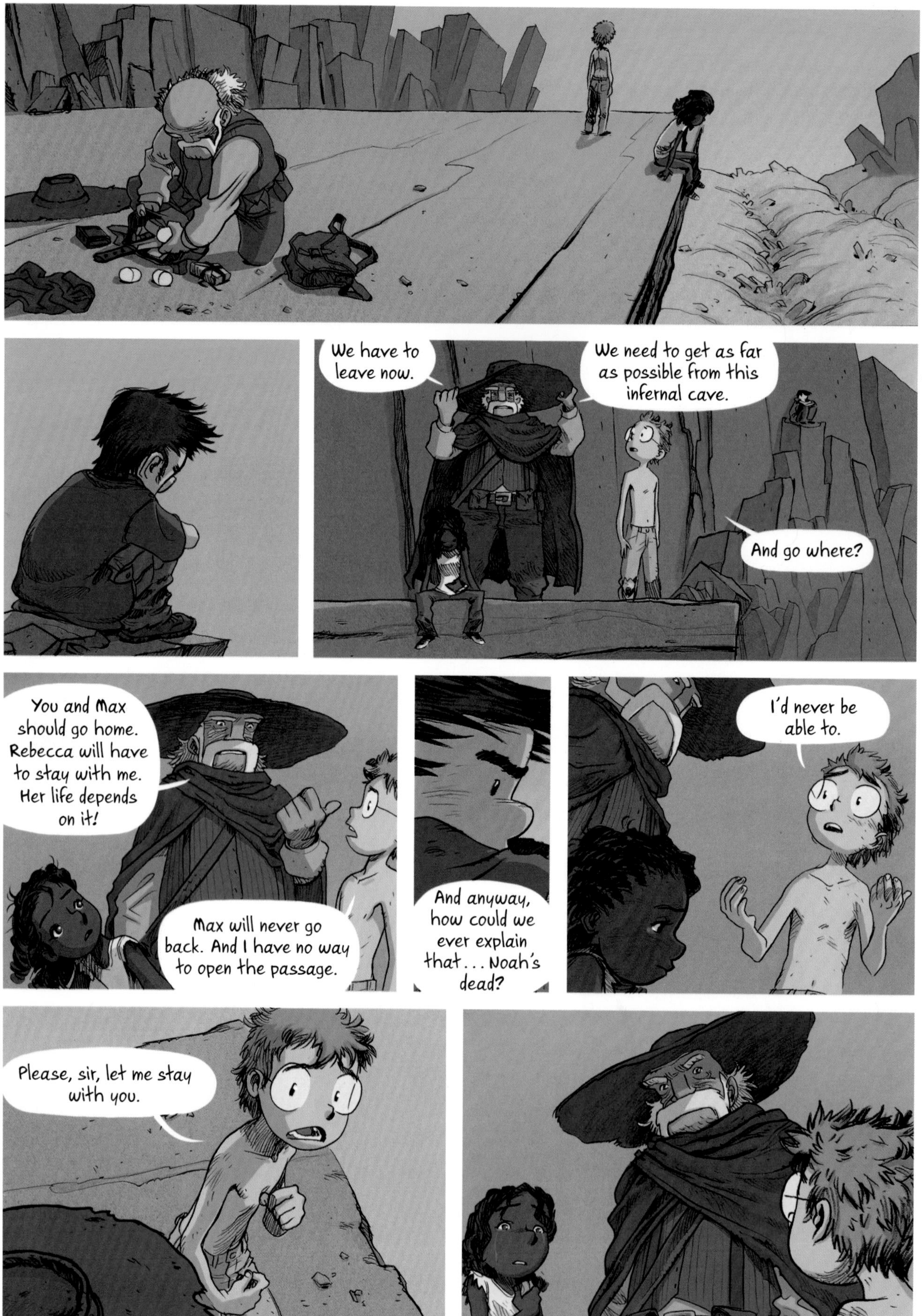

We have to leave now.
We need to get as far as possible from this infernal cave.
And go where?
You and Max should go home. Rebecca will have to stay with me. Her life depends on it!
Max will never go back. And I have no way to open the passage.
And anyway, how could we ever explain that... Noah's dead?
I'd never be able to.
Please, sir, let me stay with you.

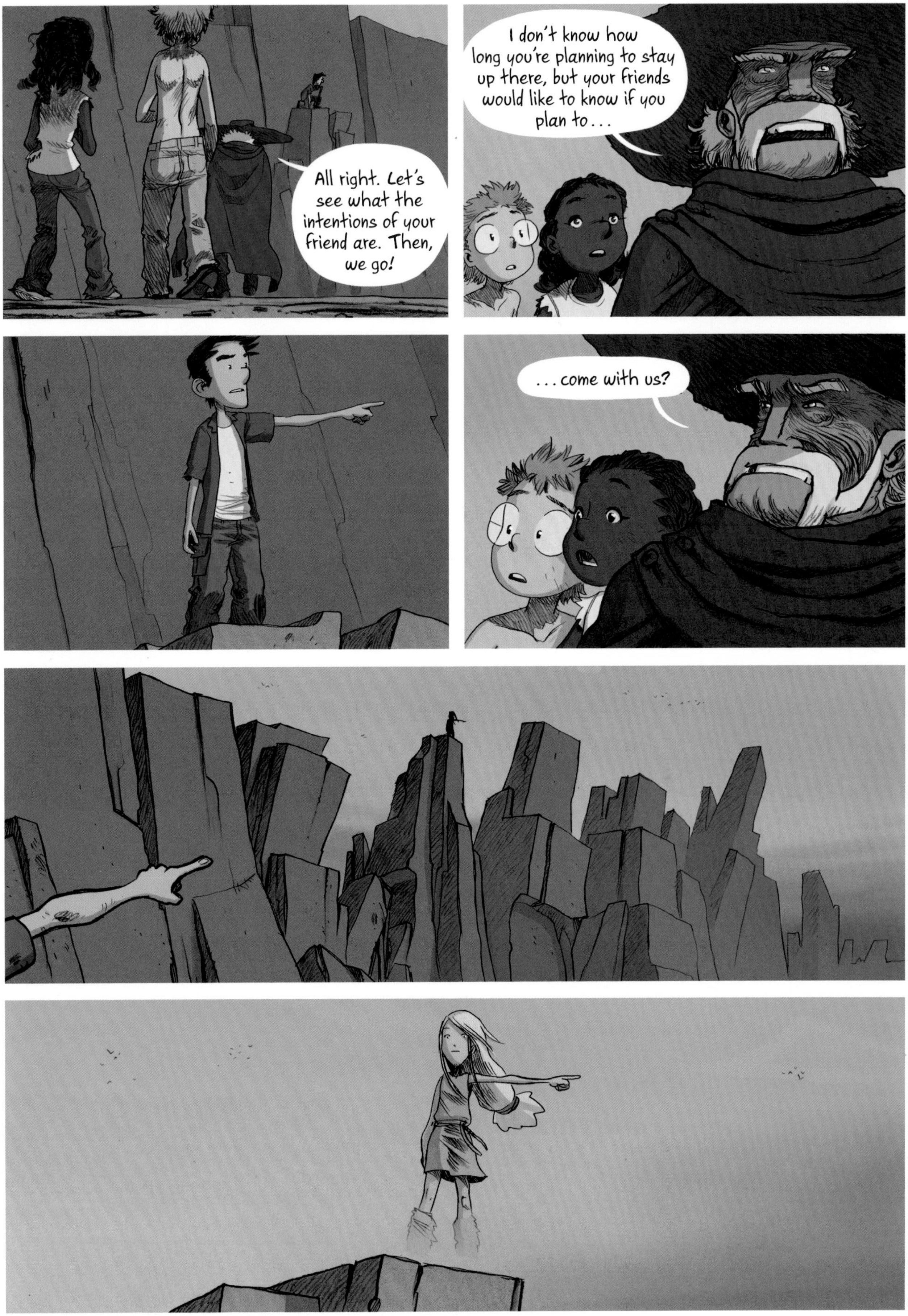
All right. Let's see what the intentions of your friend are. Then, we go!
I don't know how long you're planning to stay up there, but your friends would like to know if you plan to . . .
. . . come with us?

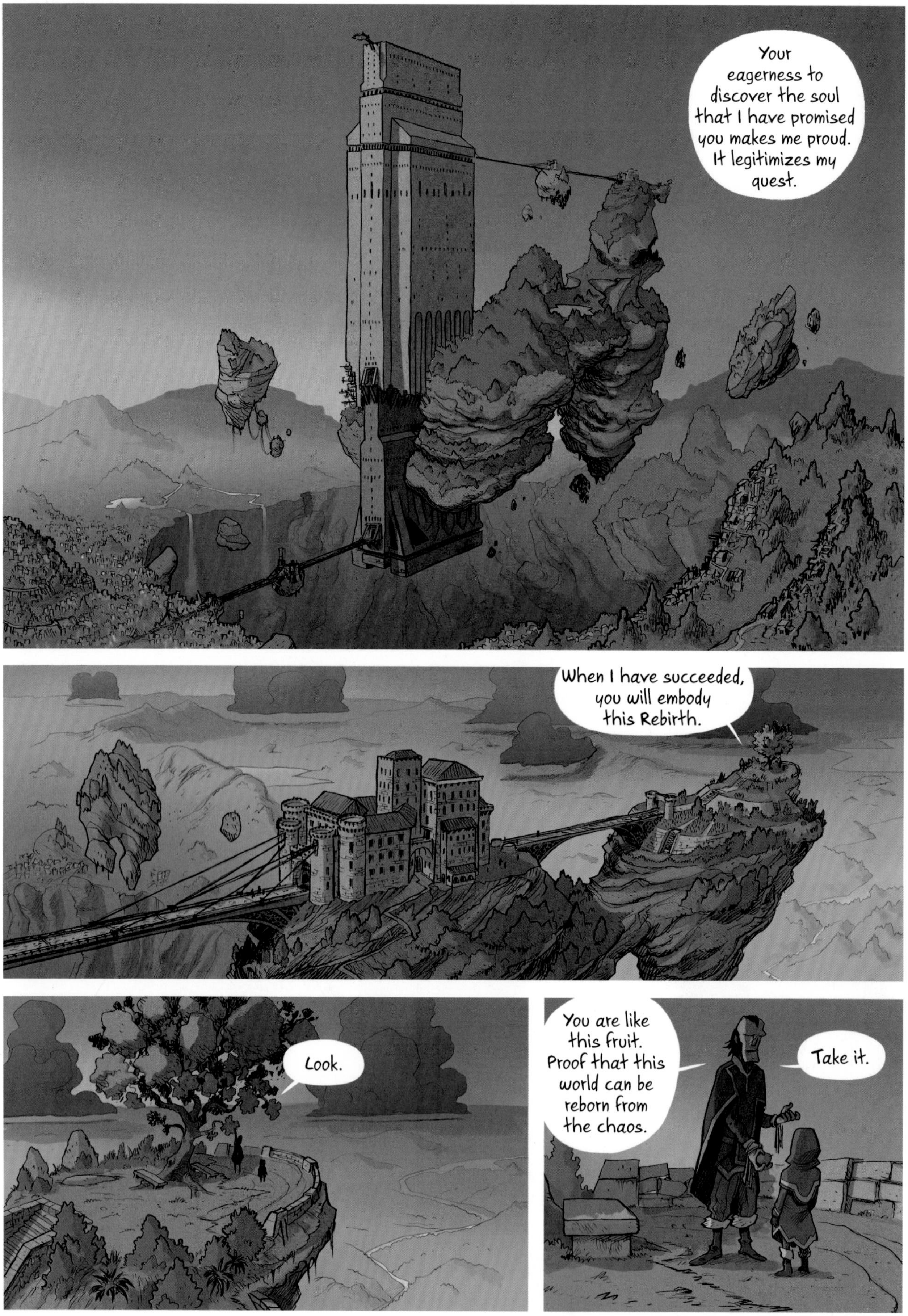
Your eagerness to discover the soul that I have promised you makes me proud. It legitimizes my quest.
When I have succeeded, you will embody this Rebirth.
Look.
You are like this fruit. Proof that this world can be reborn from the chaos.
Take it.

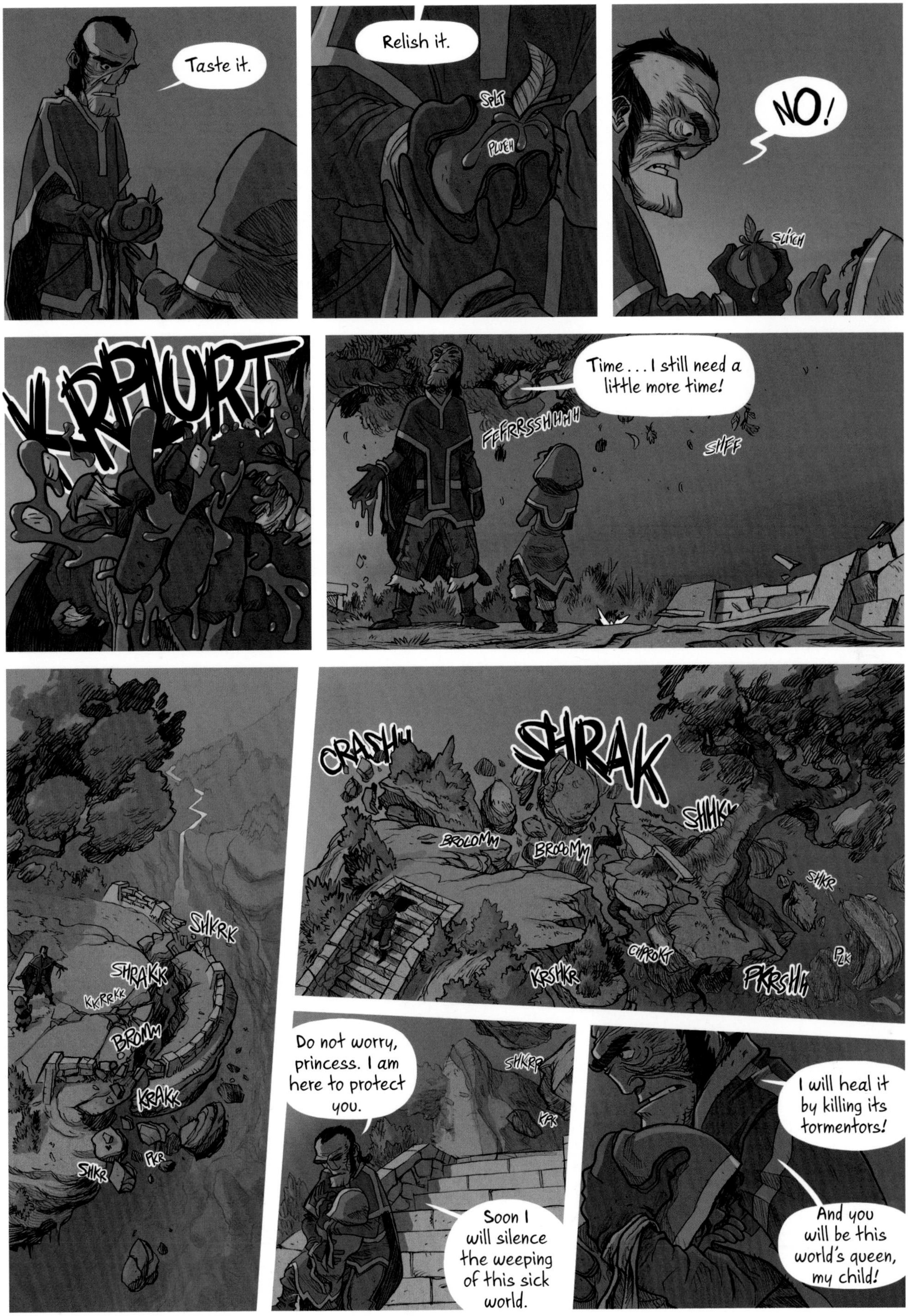

Taste it.
Relish it.
SPLT
PLTCH
NO!
SLTCH
VLRPLURT
Time . . . I still need a little more time!
FFFRRSSHMMMH
SHFF
CRASHH
SHRAK
SHHK
BROLOMM
BROOMM
SHKR
CHPROKT
KRSHKR
PKRSHK
PLK
SHRKK
SHRAKK
KKRRKK
BROMM
KRAKK
SHKR
PKR
Do not worry, princess. I am here to protect you.
SHKRR
KRK
Soon I will silence the weeping of this sick world.
I will heal it by killing its tormentors!
And you will be this world's queen, my child!

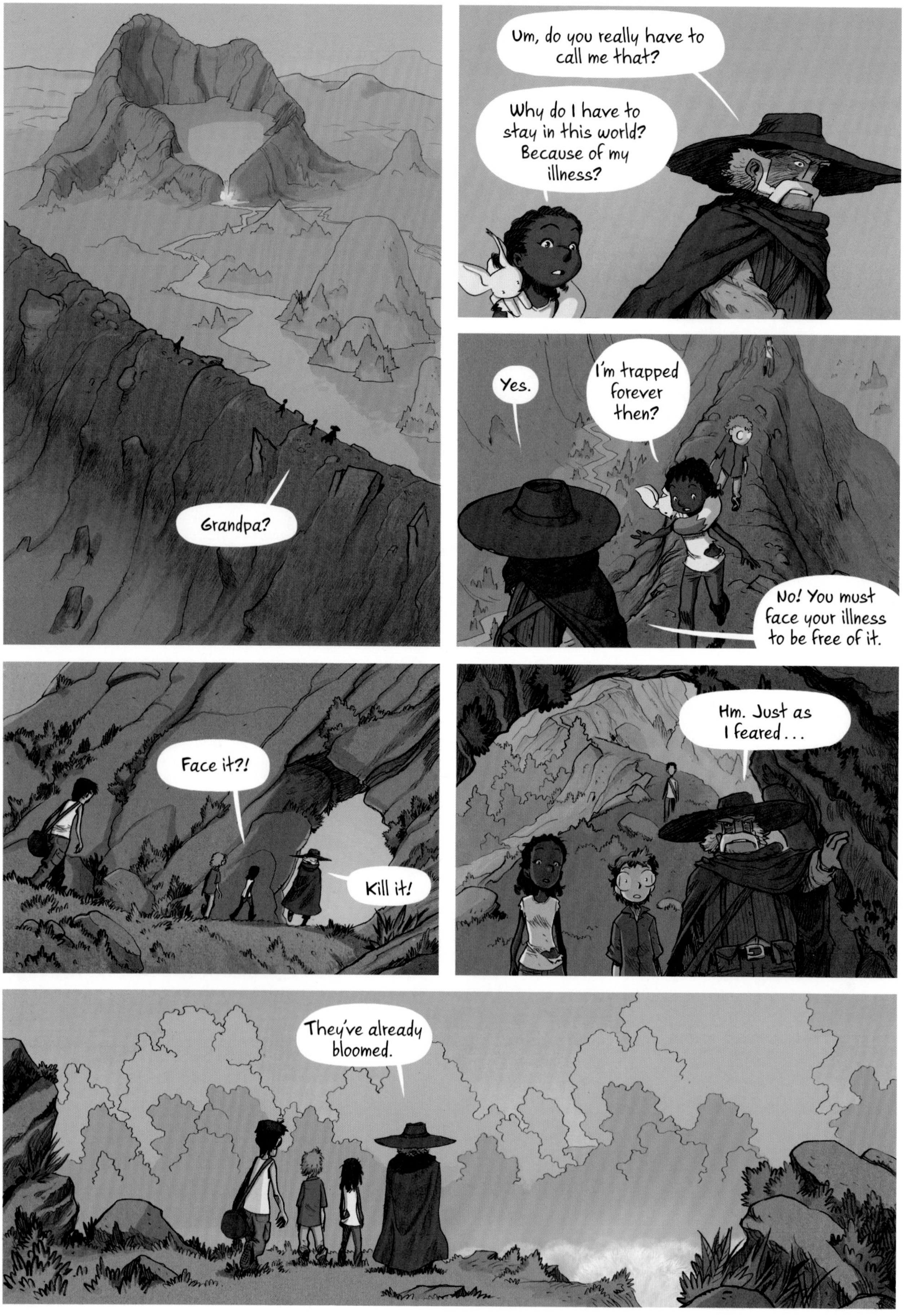
Grandpa?
Um, do you really have to call me that?
Why do I have to stay in this world? Because of my illness?
Yes.
I'm trapped forever then?
No! You must face your illness to be free of it.
Face it?!
Kill it!
Hm. Just as I feared...
They've already bloomed.

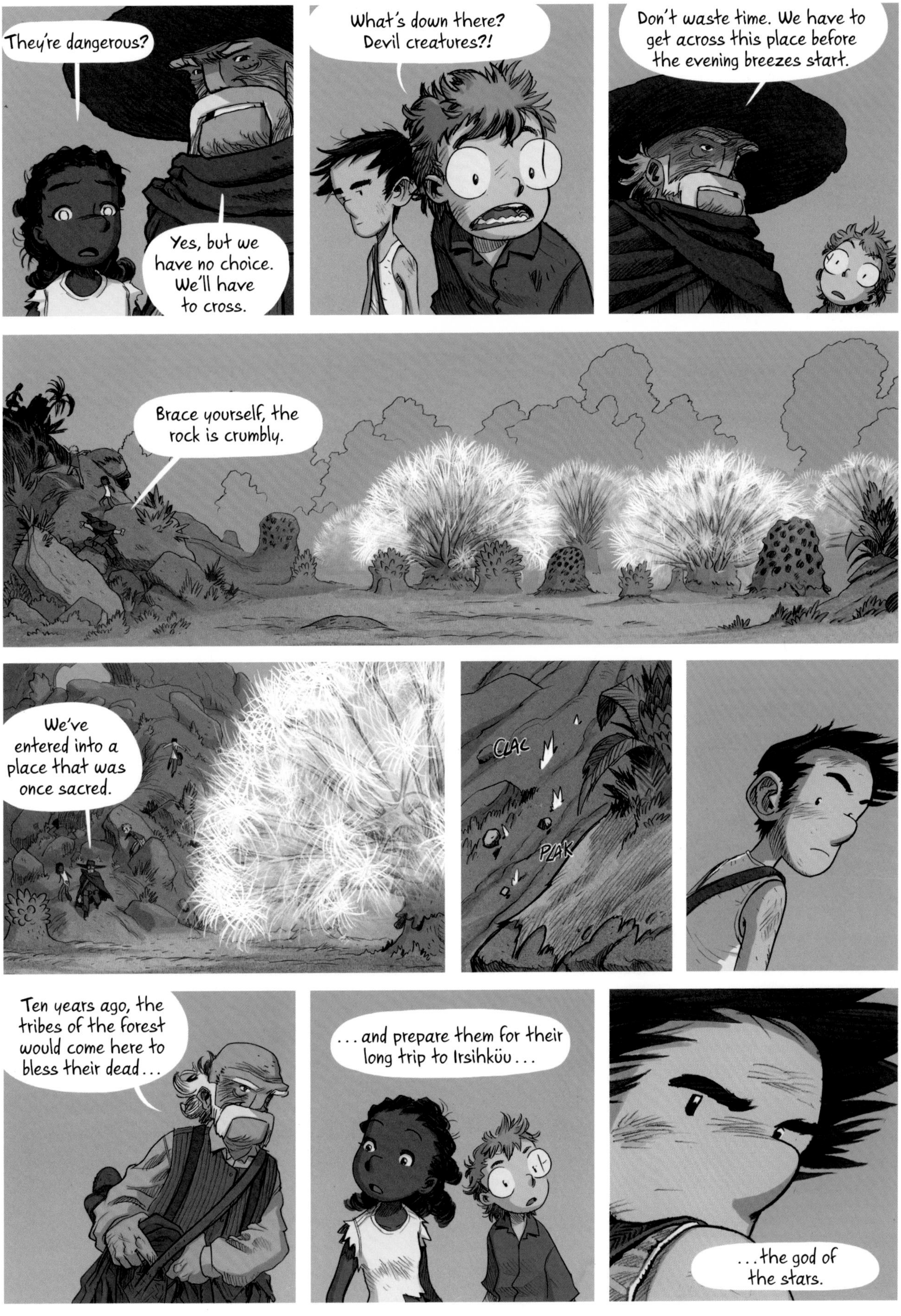
They're dangerous?
Yes, but we have no choice. We'll have to cross.
What's down there? Devil creatures?!
Don't waste time. We have to get across this place before the evening breezes start.
Brace yourself, the rock is crumbly.
We've entered into a place that was once sacred.
CLAC
PLAK
Ten years ago, the tribes of the forest would come here to bless their dead...
...and prepare them for their long trip to Irsihküu...
...the god of the stars.

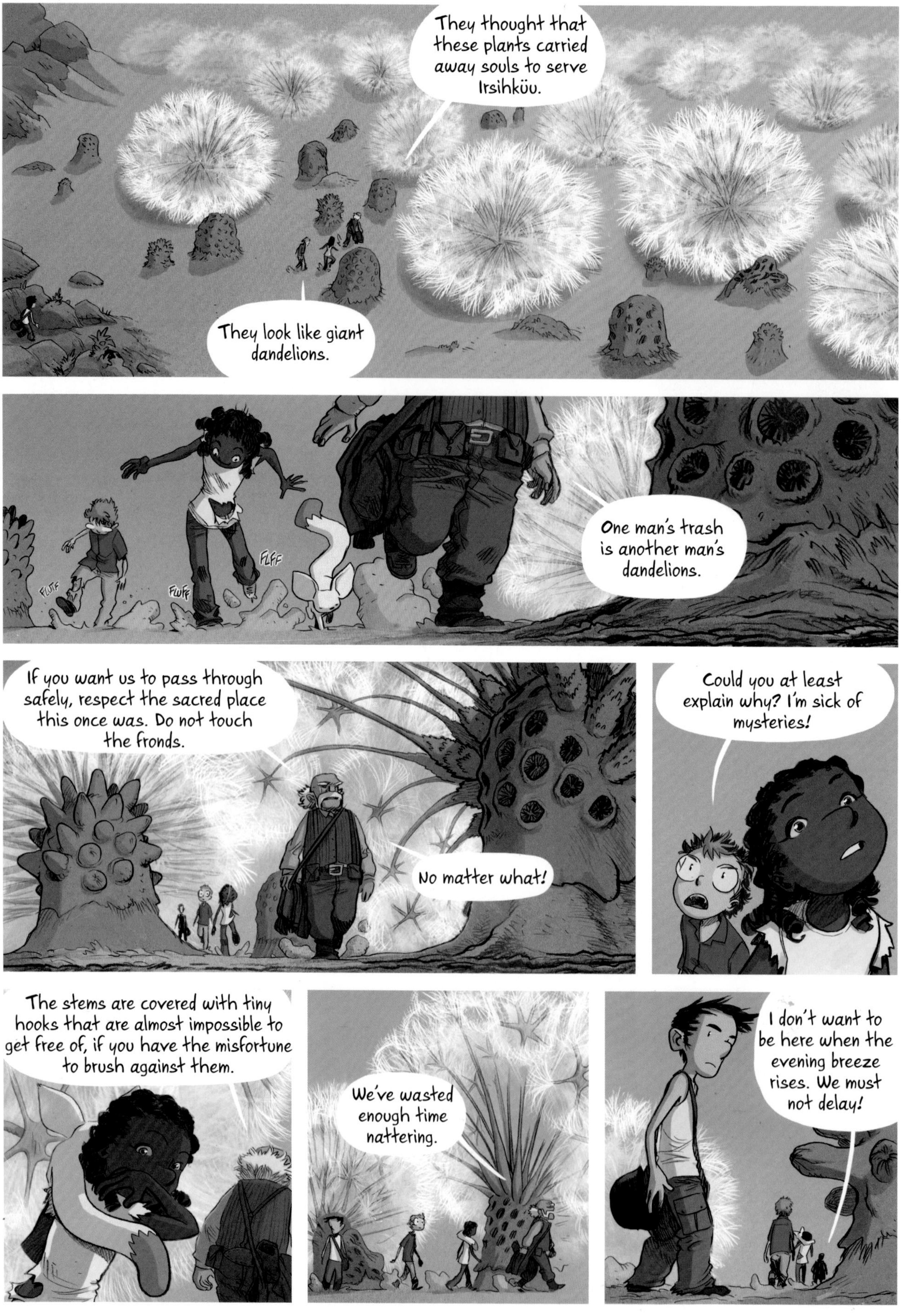
They thought that these plants carried away souls to serve Irsihküu.
They look like giant dandelions.
One man's trash is another man's dandelions.
If you want us to pass through safely, respect the sacred place this once was. Do not touch the fronds.
No matter what!
Could you at least explain why? I'm sick of mysteries!
The stems are covered with tiny hooks that are almost impossible to get free of, if you have the misfortune to brush against them.
We've wasted enough time nattering.
I don't want to be here when the evening breeze rises. We must not delay!

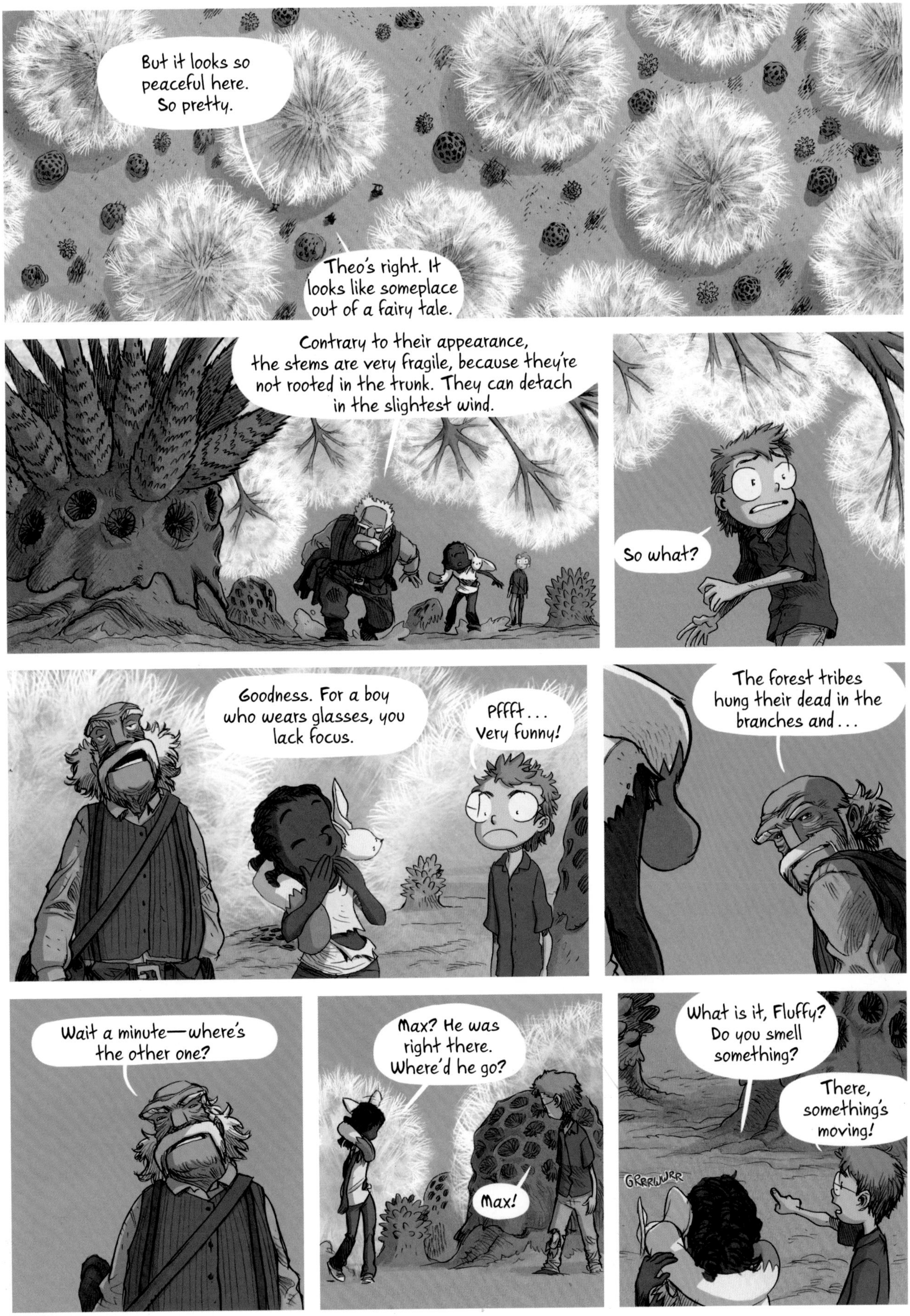

But it looks so peaceful here. So pretty.
Theo's right. It looks like someplace out of a fairy tale.
Contrary to their appearance, the stems are very fragile, because they're not rooted in the trunk. They can detach in the slightest wind.
So what?
Goodness. For a boy who wears glasses, you lack focus.
Pffft... Very funny!
The forest tribes hung their dead in the branches and...
Wait a minute—where's the other one?
Max? He was right there. Where'd he go?
Max!
What is it, Fluffy? Do you smell something?
There, something's moving!
GRRRWWRR

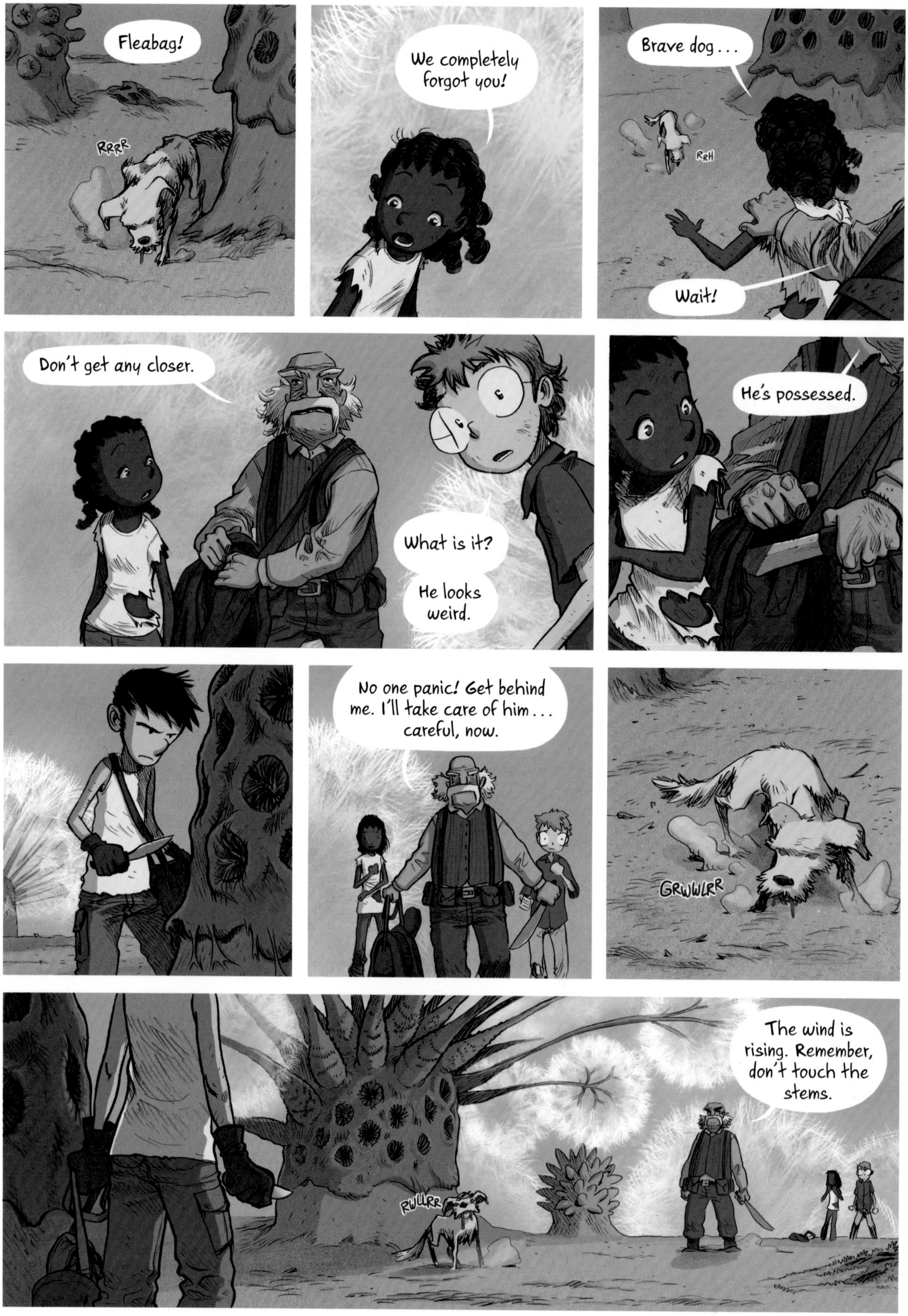
Fleabag!
RRRR
We completely forgot you!
Brave dog . . .
RRH
Wait!
Don't get any closer.
What is it?
He looks weird.
He's possessed.
No one panic! Get behind me. I'll take care of him . . . careful, now.
GRWWLRR
RWLLRR
The wind is rising. Remember, don't touch the stems.

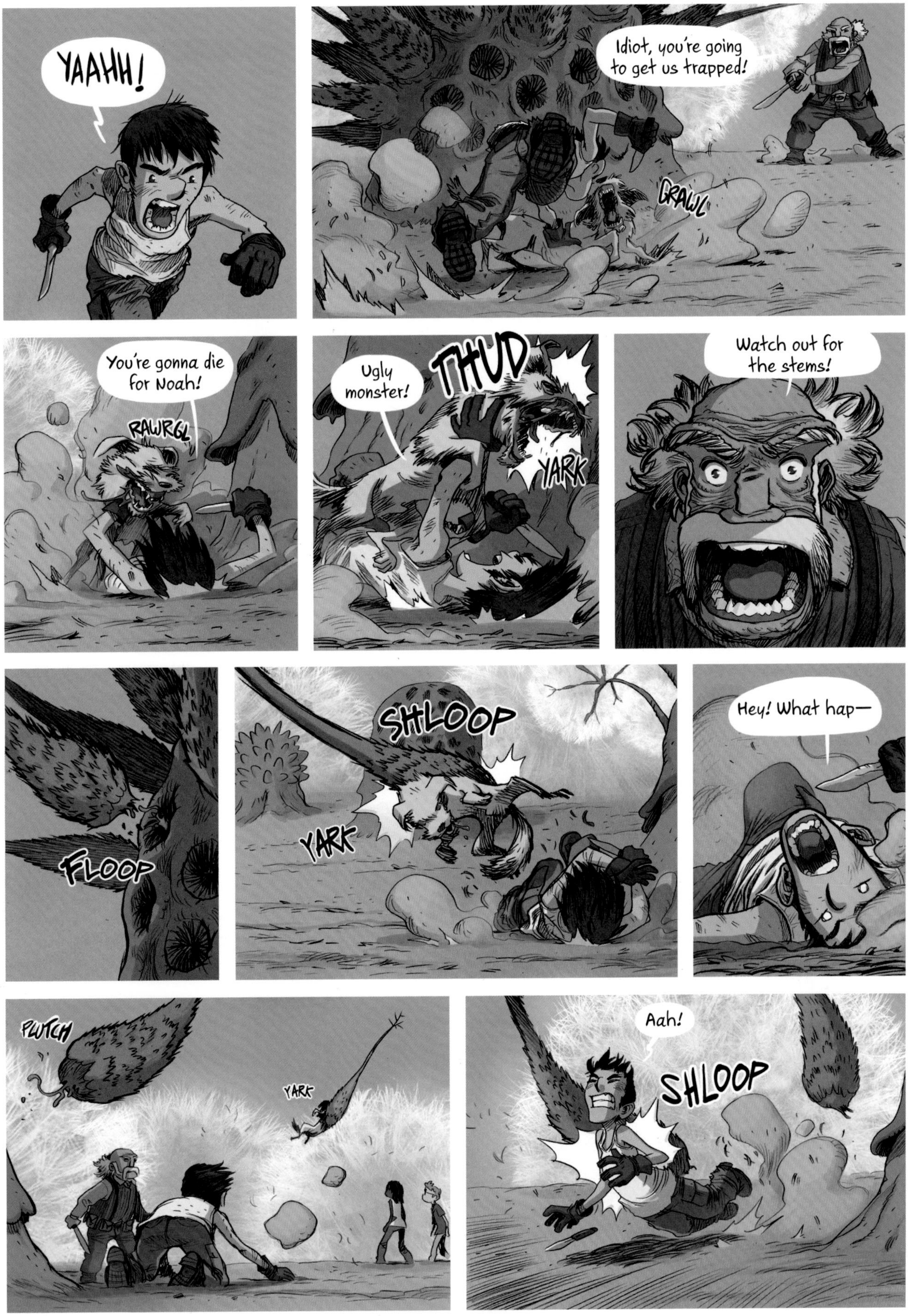
YAAHH!
Idiot, you're going to get us trapped!
GRAWL
You're gonna die for Noah!
RAWRGL
Ugly monster!
THUD
YARK
Watch out for the stems!
FLOOP
SHLOOP
YARK
Hey! What hap—
PLUTCH
YARK
Aah!
SHLOOP

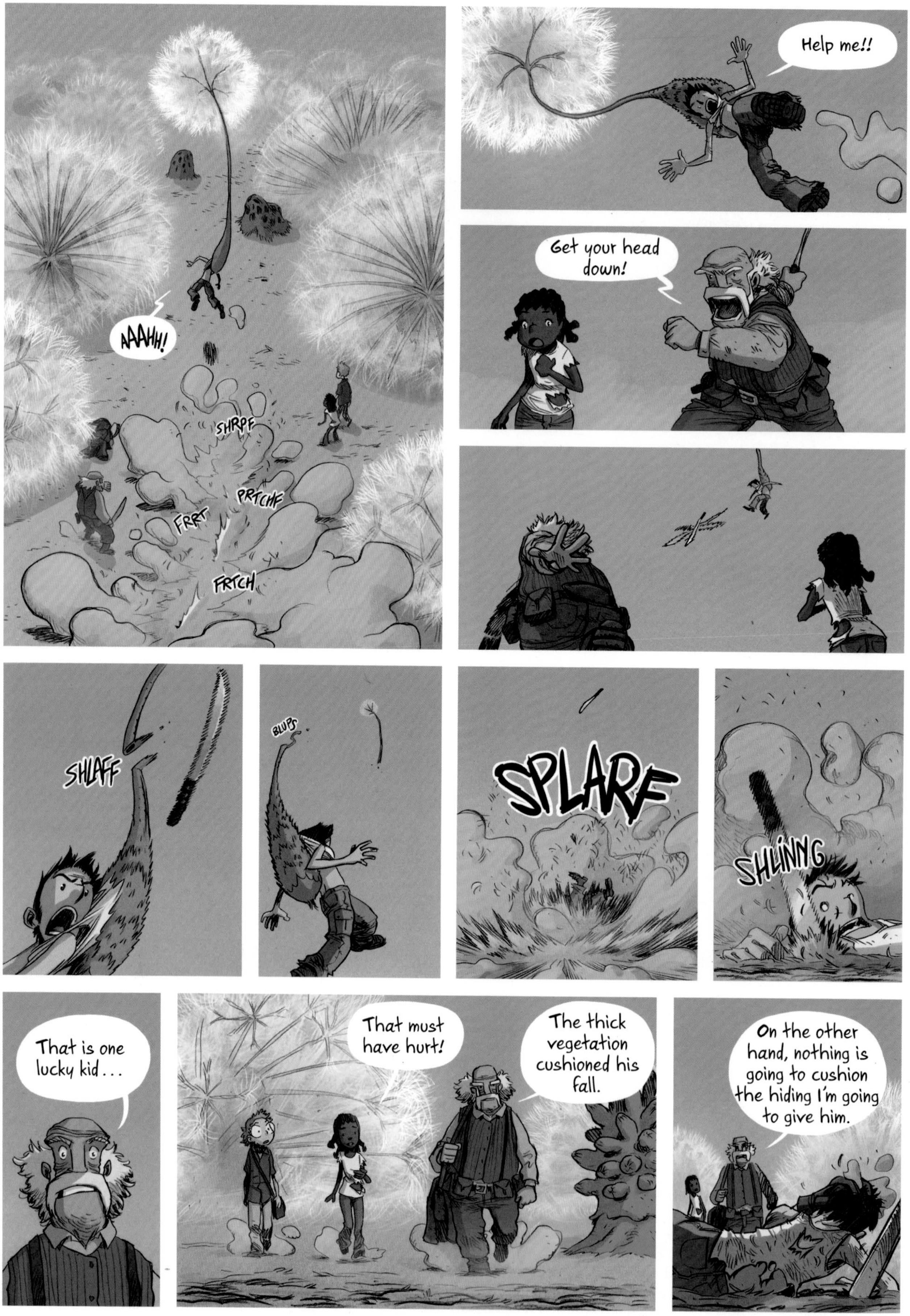
AAAHH!
SHRPF
PRTCHF
FRRT
FRTCH
Help me!!
Get your head down!
SHLAFF
BLUPS
SPLARF
SHLINNG
That is one lucky kid . . .
That must have hurt!
The thick vegetation cushioned his fall.
On the other hand, nothing is going to cushion the hiding I'm going to give him.

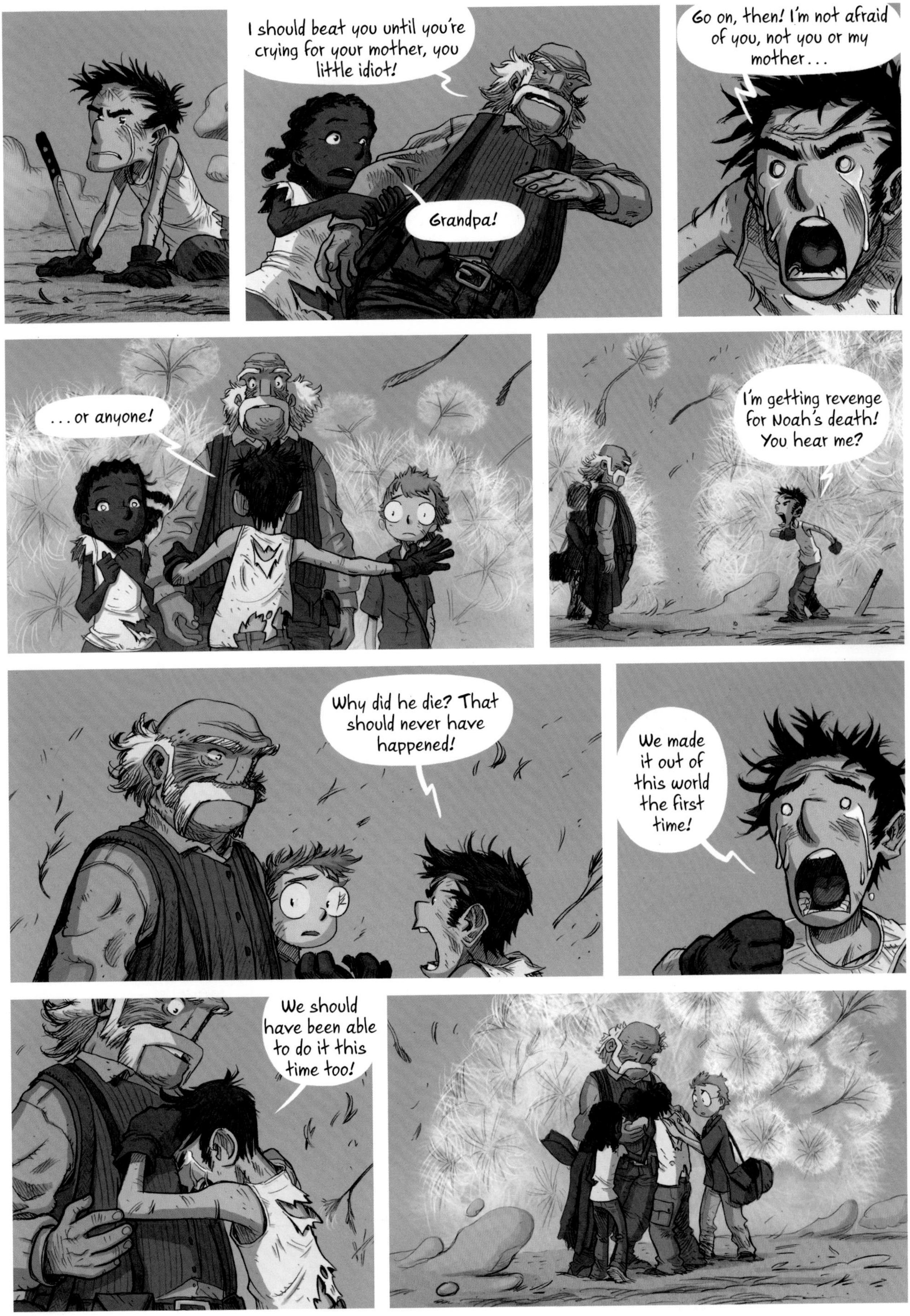
I should beat you until you're crying for your mother, you little idiot!
Grandpa!
Go on, then! I'm not afraid of you, not you or my mother...
...or anyone!
I'm getting revenge for Noah's death! You hear me?
Why did he die? That should never have happened!
We made it out of this world the first time!
We should have been able to do it this time too!

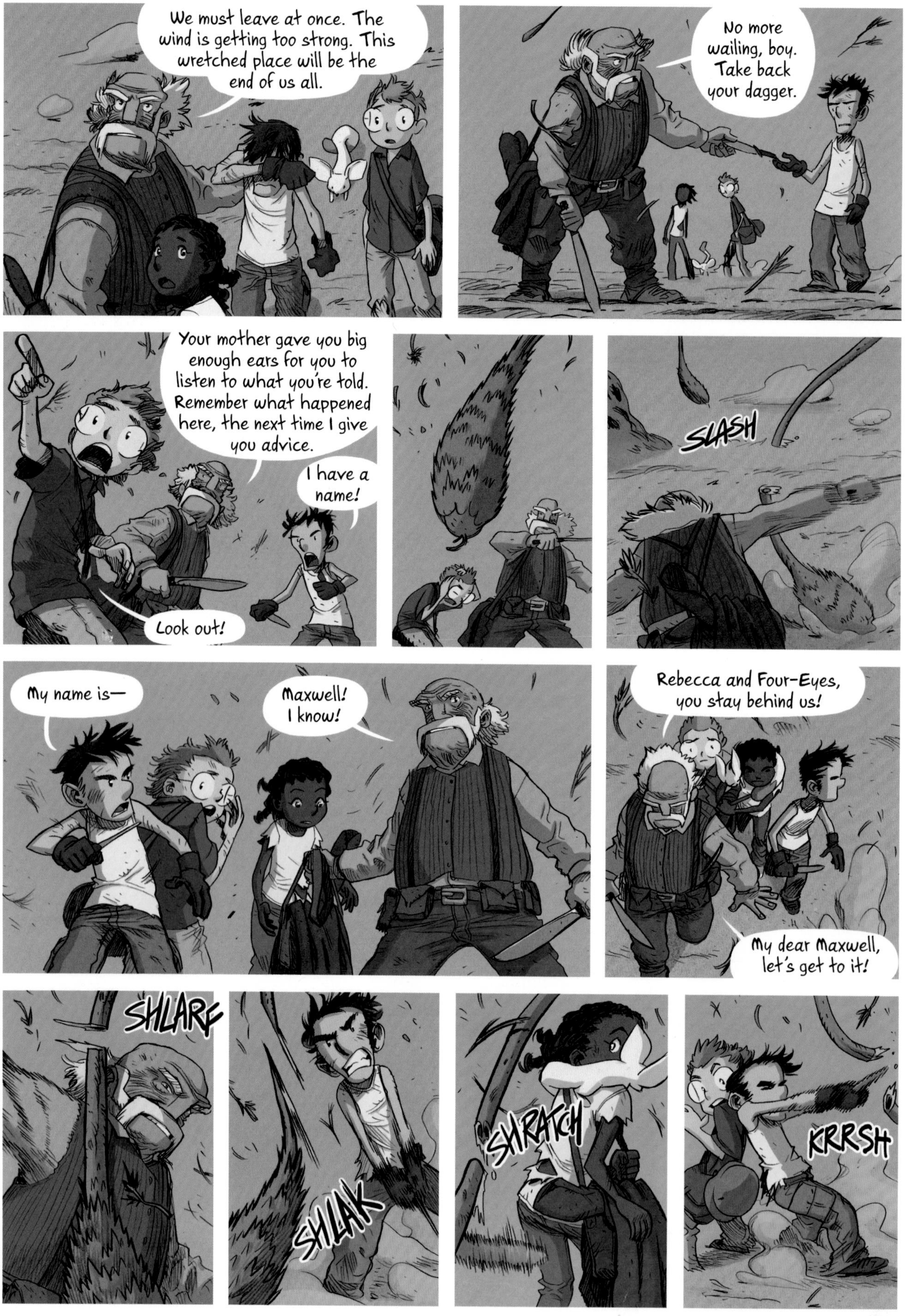
We must leave at once. The wind is getting too strong. This wretched place will be the end of us all.
No more wailing, boy. Take back your dagger.
Your mother gave you big enough ears for you to listen to what you're told. Remember what happened here, the next time I give you advice.
I have a name!
Look out!
SLASH
My name is—
Maxwell! I know!
Rebecca and Four-Eyes, you stay behind us!
My dear Maxwell, let's get to it!
SHLARF
SHLAK
SHRATCH
KRRSH

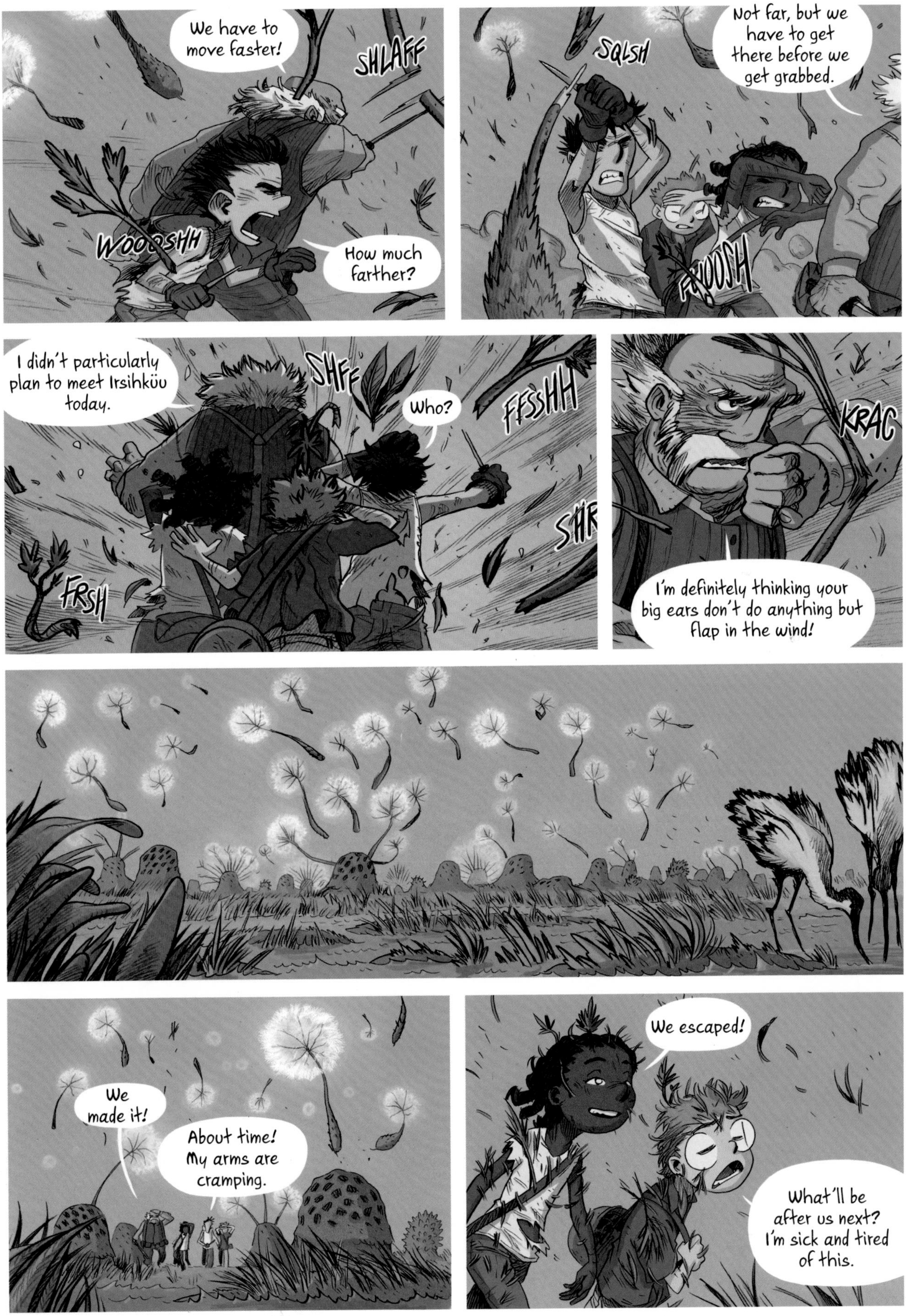
We have to move faster!
SHLAFF
WOOOSHH
How much farther?
SQLSH
Not far, but we have to get there before we get grabbed.
FWOOSH
I didn't particularly plan to meet Irsihküu today.
SHFF
Who?
FFSSHH
SHR
FRSH
KRAC
I'm definitely thinking your big ears don't do anything but flap in the wind!
We made it!
About time! My arms are cramping.
We escaped!
What'll be after us next? I'm sick and tired of this.

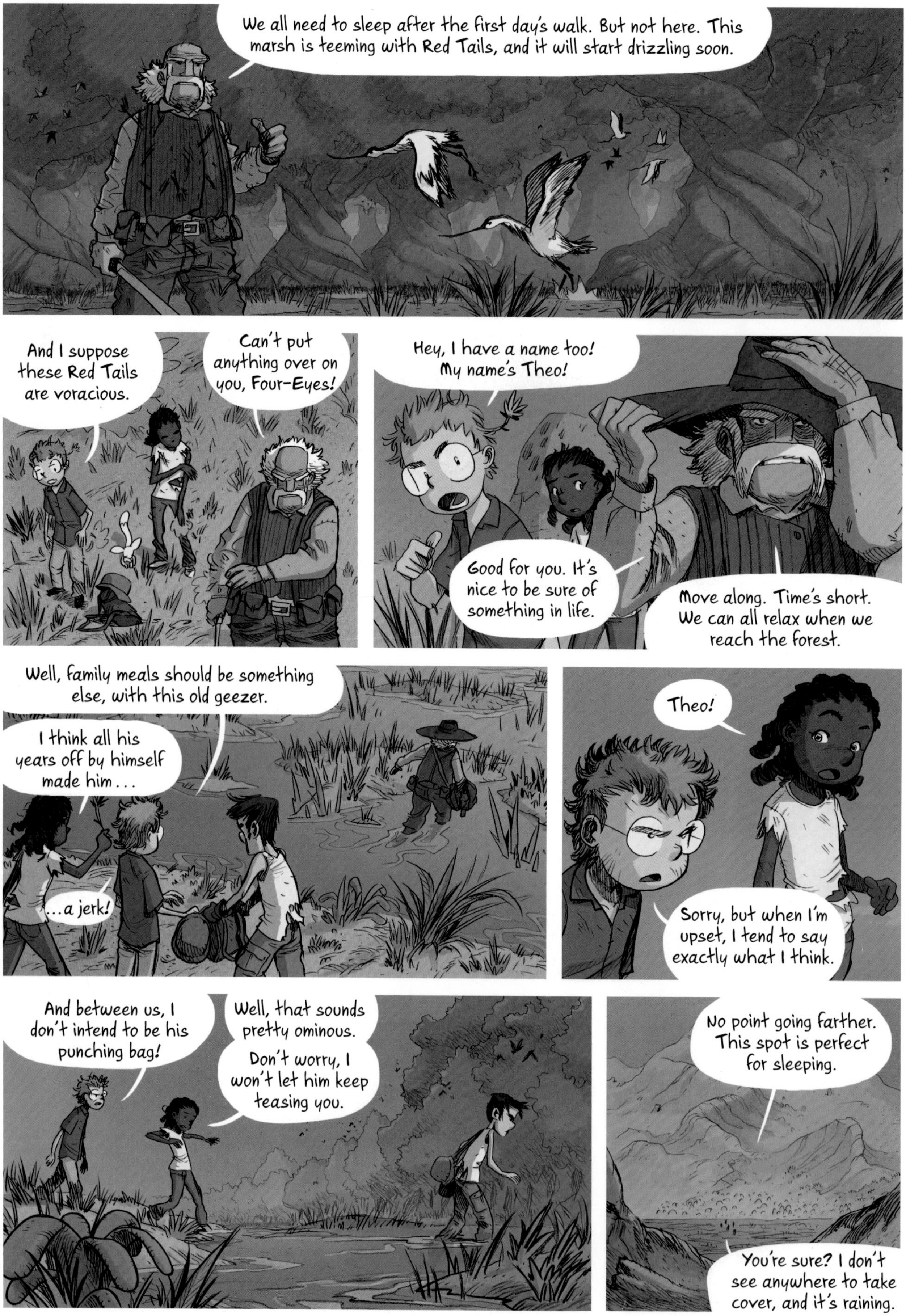
We all need to sleep after the first day's walk. But not here. This marsh is teeming with Red Tails, and it will start drizzling soon.
And I suppose these Red Tails are voracious.
Can't put anything over on you, Four-Eyes!
Hey, I have a name too! My name's Theo!
Good for you. It's nice to be sure of something in life.
Move along. Time's short. We can all relax when we reach the forest.
Well, family meals should be something else, with this old geezer.
I think all his years off by himself made him . . .
. . . a jerk!
Theo!
Sorry, but when I'm upset, I tend to say exactly what I think.
And between us, I don't intend to be his punching bag!
Well, that sounds pretty ominous.
Don't worry, I won't let him keep teasing you.
No point going farther. This spot is perfect for sleeping.
You're sure? I don't see anywhere to take cover, and it's raining.

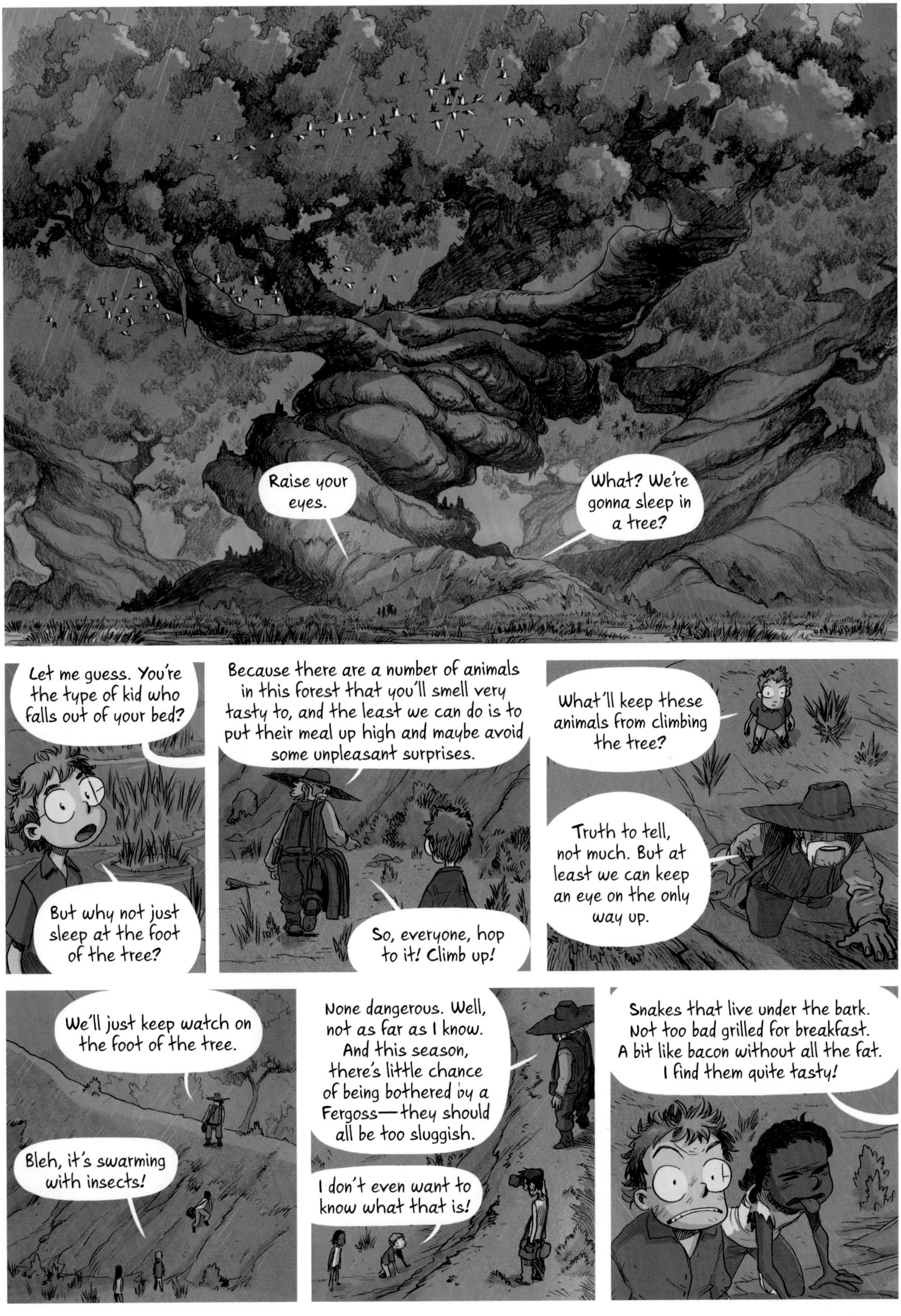
Raise your eyes.
What? We're gonna sleep in a tree?
Let me guess. You're the type of kid who falls out of your bed?
But why not just sleep at the foot of the tree?
Because there are a number of animals in this forest that you'll smell very tasty to, and the least we can do is to put their meal up high and maybe avoid some unpleasant surprises.
So, everyone, hop to it! Climb up!
What'll keep these animals from climbing the tree?
Truth to tell, not much. But at least we can keep an eye on the only way up.
We'll just keep watch on the foot of the tree.
Bleh, it's swarming with insects!
None dangerous. Well, not as far as I know. And this season, there's little chance of being bothered by a Fergoss—they should all be too sluggish.
I don't even want to know what that is!
Snakes that live under the bark. Not too bad grilled for breakfast. A bit like bacon without all the fat. I find them quite tasty!

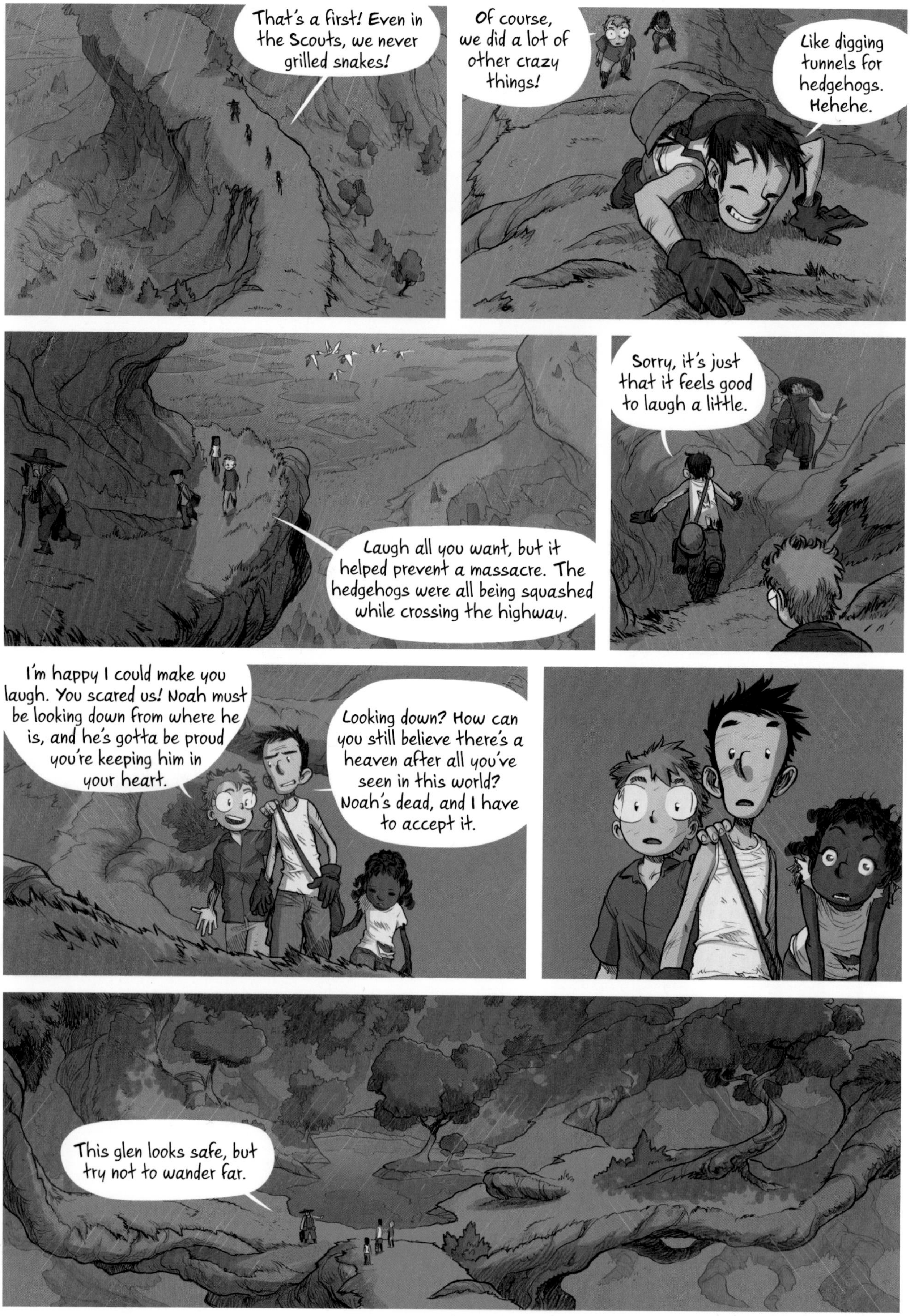
That's a first! Even in the Scouts, we never grilled snakes!
Of course, we did a lot of other crazy things!
Like digging tunnels for hedgehogs. Hehehe.
Laugh all you want, but it helped prevent a massacre. The hedgehogs were all being squashed while crossing the highway.
Sorry, it's just that it feels good to laugh a little.
I'm happy I could make you laugh. You scared us! Noah must be looking down from where he is, and he's gotta be proud you're keeping him in your heart.
Looking down? How can you still believe there's a heaven after all you've seen in this world? Noah's dead, and I have to accept it.
This glen looks safe, but try not to wander far.

I'm sorry about your friend. This world wasn't made for children. It's all my fault.

Why would you say that? I'm the one who led the boys here. If Noah is dead, it's my fault.

Maybe, but I'm responsible for the chaos that prevails in this world.

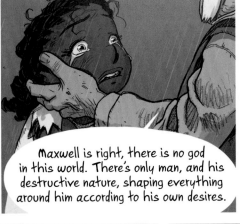

Maxwell is right, there is no god in this world. There's only man, and his destructive nature, shaping everything around him according to his own desires.

Don't say that, Grandpa!

I'm saying the truth. I created the Master of Shadows, just as I created the myths of this world. Soon you'll understand.

I thought I was a god.

And as such, I destroyed this paradise.

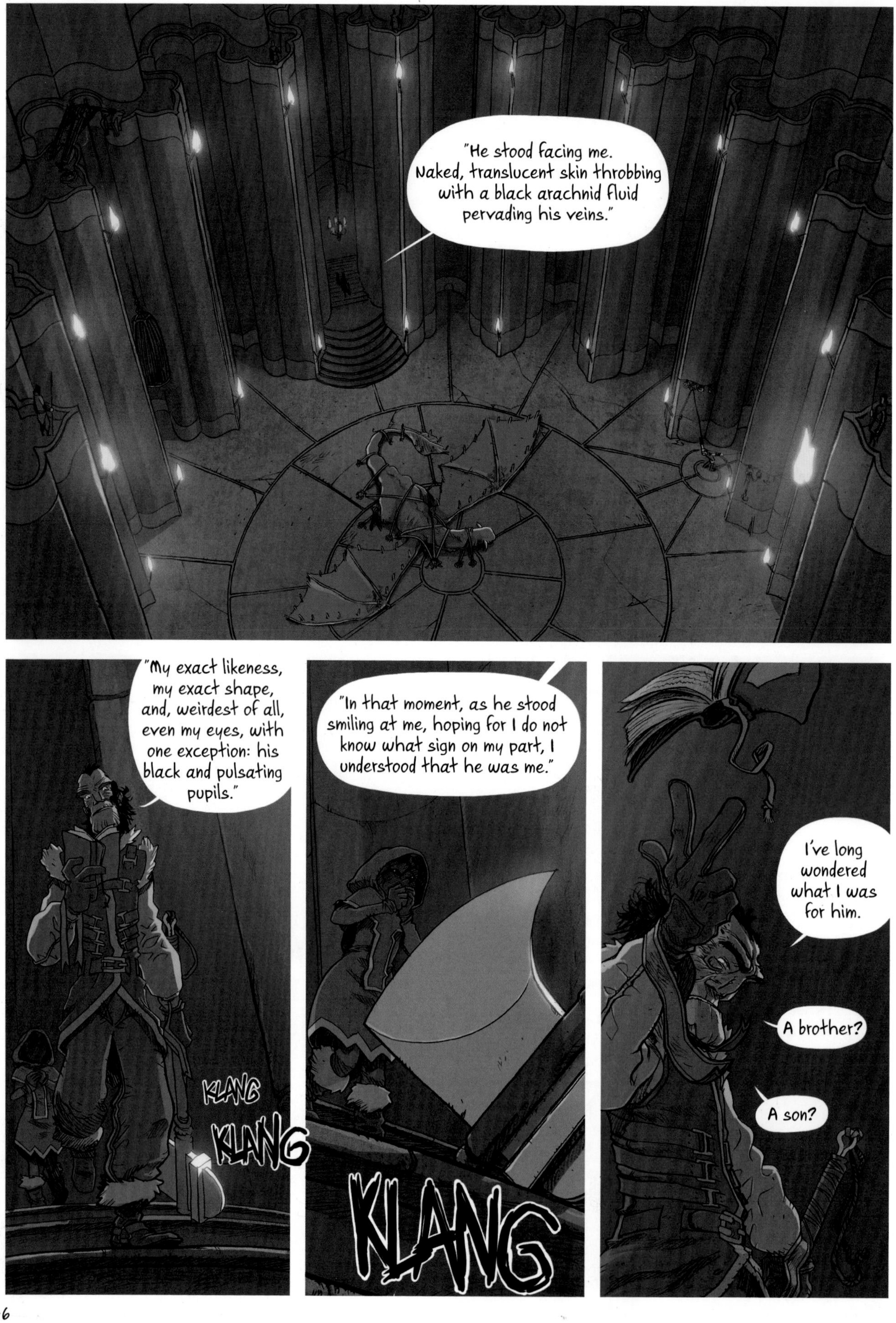
"He stood facing me. Naked, translucent skin throbbing with a black arachnid fluid pervading his veins."
"My exact likeness, my exact shape, and, weirdest of all, even my eyes, with one exception: his black and pulsating pupils."
KLANG
KLANG
"In that moment, as he stood smiling at me, hoping for I do not know what sign on my part, I understood that he was me."
KLANG
I've long wondered what I was for him.
A brother?
A son?

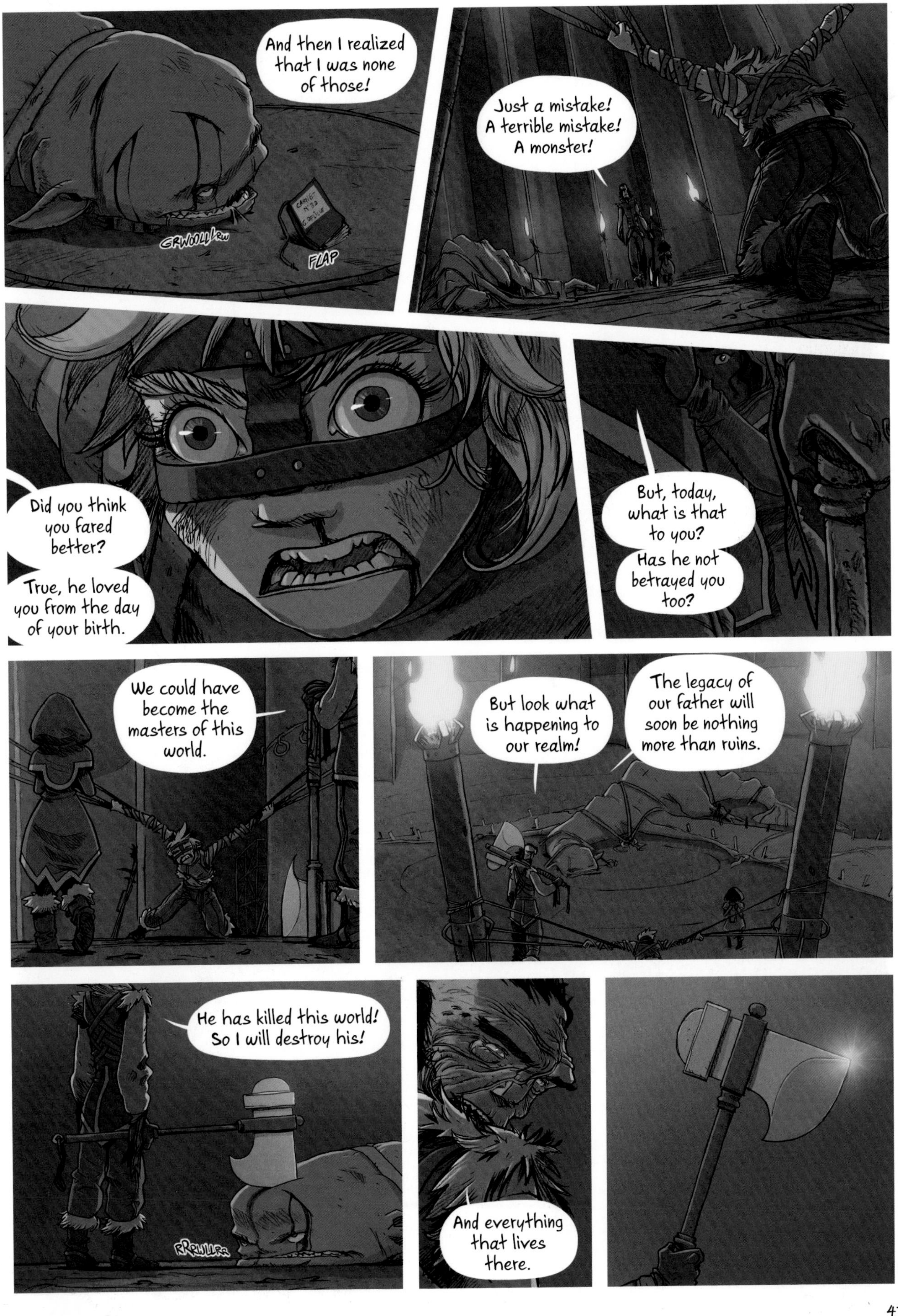
And then I realized that I was none of those!
GRWOOLLLRW
FLAP
Just a mistake! A terrible mistake! A monster!
Did you think you fared better?
True, he loved you from the day of your birth.
But, today, what is that to you?
Has he not betrayed you too?
We could have become the masters of this world.
But look what is happening to our realm!
The legacy of our father will soon be nothing more than ruins.
He has killed this world! So I will destroy his!
RRRWLLRR
And everything that lives there.

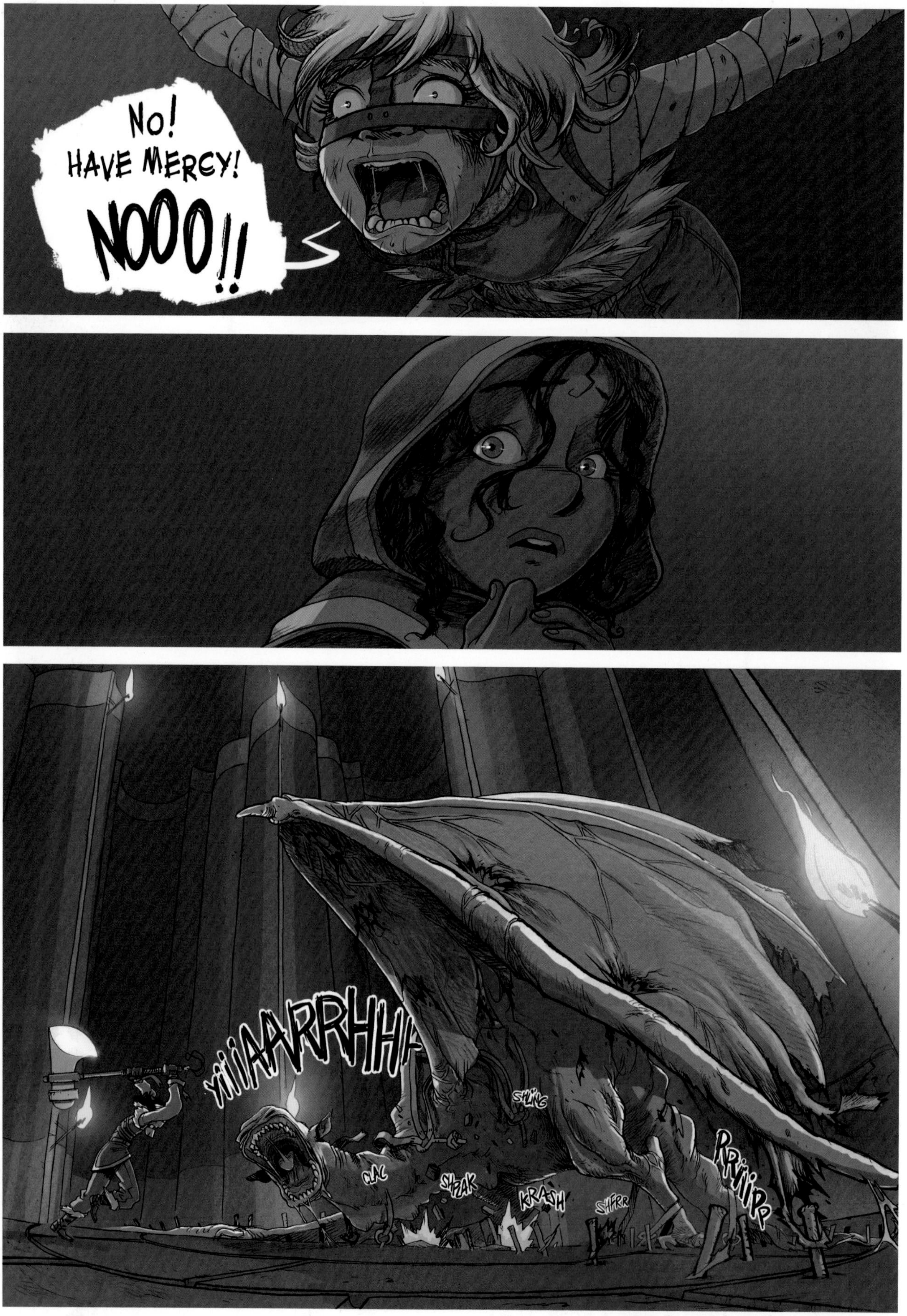
No! HAVE MERCY! NOOO!!
YIIIAARRHHH
SHLING
CLAC
SHRAK
KRASH
SHFRR
RRVIIIPP

To be continued...

Art by Bannister
Story by Nykko
Colors by Jaffré
Translation by Carol Klio Burrell

First American edition published in 2011 by Graphic Universe™.
Published by arrangement with S.A. DUPUIS, Belgium.

Graphic Universe™
A division of Lerner Publishing Group, Inc.
241 First Avenue North
Minneapolis, MN 55401 U.S.A.

Website address: www.lernerbooks.com

Library of Congress Cataloging-in-Publication Data

Bannister.
The parting / art by Bannister ; story by Nykko. — 1st American ed.
p. cm. — (ElseWhere chronicles ; bk. 5)
Summary: Max returns to ElseWhere to rescue his friends Noah, Theo, and
Rebecca, whose quest to find a cure for Rebecca's mysterious illness has
led them into a dangerous cave populated by creatures trapped between
living and Shadow.
ISBN: 978-0-7613-6632-4 (lib. bdg. : alk. paper)
1. Graphic novels. [1. Graphic novels. 2. Horror stories.] I. Nykko. II. Title.
PZ7.7.B34Par 2011
741.5'973—dc22   2011004992

Manufactured in the United States of America
1 – DP – 7/15/11

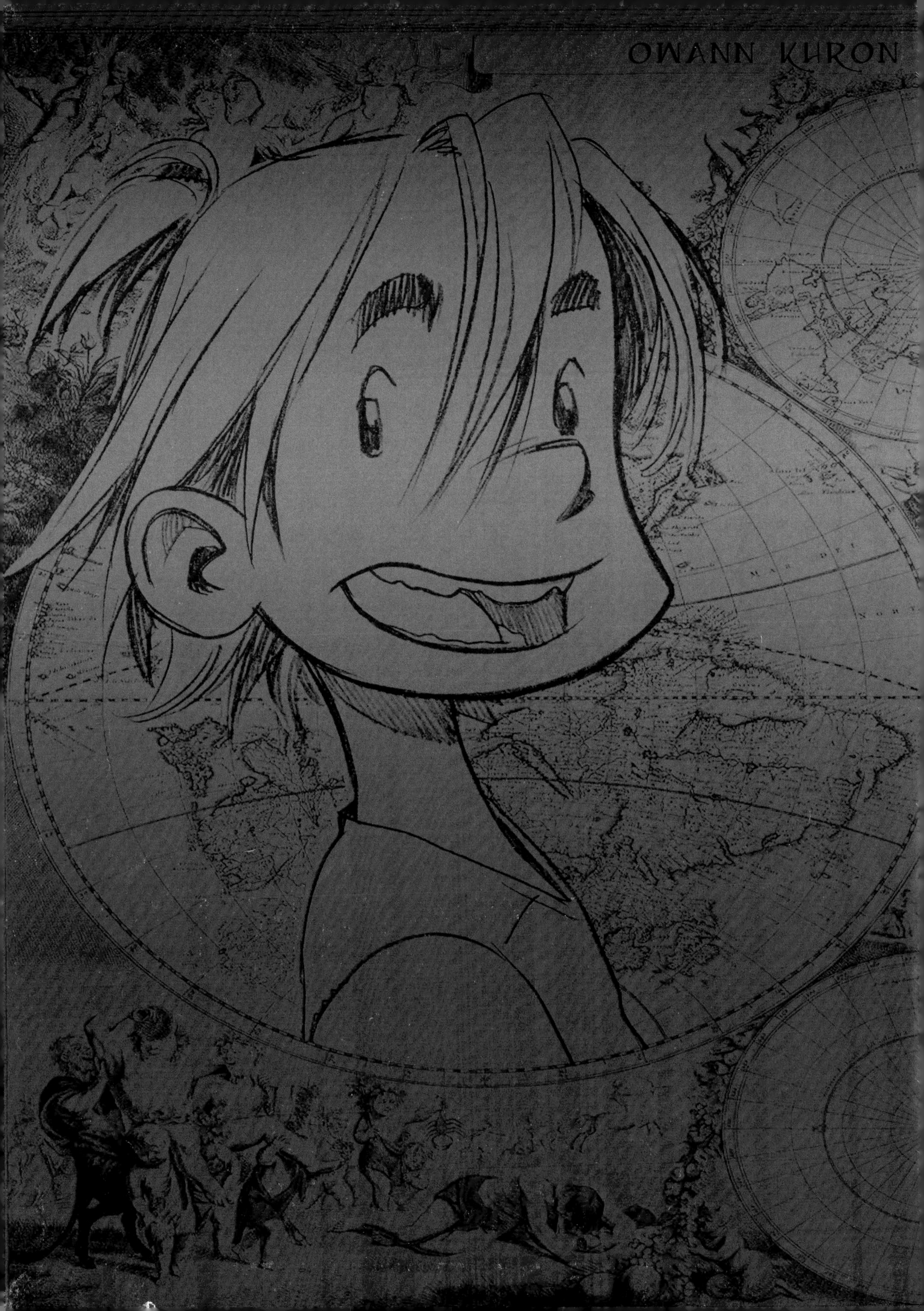
OWANN KHRON